I0701308

The Witch
And Other Tales of the American Gothic

Written by
Jessica Hobbs

Artwork by
Hannah Park

Layout Design by
Ian Gifford

Cover Art by
Elias Armao

ISBN: 979-8-9879389-0-4

Library of Congress Control Number: 2023906909

For Robin

*My best friend, my biggest fan, and the man whose love
for my gothic sensibilities inspired this book.
I love you.*

Contents

The Witch......................1

The Debutante...............33

The Acrobat..................55

The Immigrant...............83

The Lumberjack...........109

The Miner..................131

The Psychiatrist...........149

The Witch
And Other Tales of the American Gothic

A Collection of Short Stories by
Jessica Hobbs

The Witch

Portland, ME

1814

T he stone cottage was small, but filled with warmth and everything else the Witch could need: a cot, a rocking chair, a fireplace, an iron skillet for cooking, a lush garden full of roses, vegetables, and dozens of herbs, and various animal pelts hanging on the walls, waiting to be sewn into blankets and wool dresses for the long, harsh New England winters.

But though the Witch had become quite skilled at gardening and trapping in order to survive alone in the woods of Maine, her life in exile was not one of her choosing. It was a weight the Witch carried with her every day.

As a child, the Witch had one true friend by the name of Mary Grace, and many solitary hours in the woods were consumed by thoughts of her and the happier times they had spent together playing near the ocean, picking flowers in her mother's garden, or even completing household chores.

The two had longed to be sisters through the entirety of their childhood, and they nearly got their wish at the ages of fifteen, when the Witch's mother passed away after years of agonizing illness. Her grieving father, a fisherman by trade, set sail shortly after, leaving his only daughter in the care of Mary Grace's parents. He never returned.

Though the family had been kind to her, the burden her presence had placed upon them was obvious. Thus, the Witch began to accept the inevitability of marriage.

And that is where our story begins.

* * *

The Witch was not known as such when she was young. Before the tragedy, she was a normal girl of a somewhat shy disposition, with strawberry hair that hung in waves around her face and eyes that matched the grey of the early New England mornings.

Mary Grace was a beautiful child, and the only child in the village not entirely of English decent. Mary Grace's father had been a trader for many years, and during one particularly fruitful expedition, had met and fallen madly in love with a woman from Siam. It was said that the young man was so taken with her he had renegotiated the terms of his trade heavily in favor of the local merchant, forfeiting a sizable amount of money in order to impress her father. Once her family gave their blessing, the two were married in Siam before embarking upon their journey back to Portland.

The love story shared between Mary Grace's parents was more exciting than anything she had ever read in a book or heard in church sermon. Someday, she believed, her own father would bring her with him on one of his excursions at sea. Perhaps they would sail so far from home they could discover an exciting new land, where she would meet a nice young man who would introduce her to customs, languages, and delicacies she could not yet imagine.

The people of the town didn't think much about her at all, really, until the news of her mother's illness. Even before she had become bedridden, Mother had stopped attending church, and quiet murmurs began to spread around town that she had given up on God, her declining health providing evidence of God's anger toward her for such blasphemy. On one occasion, the family had awoken to a group of men pounding on the front door. Before Mother ushered her back to bed, she could hear the accusations being thrown at Father: that he had allowed Satan to enter his home, abandoning his duty as the man of the house to protect his family, and must repent for his misdeeds before evil could be allowed to infect the entire town.

The death of her mother and disappearance of her father caused the rumors to become much more vicious.

Though some of the neighbors cast judgment upon Mary Grace's parents for accepting her, most agreed that the child being raised by a God-fearing family was best for her and for the spiritual health of the community.

A few of them looked upon the girl with pity once she became an orphan, but motherless children were hardly rare, as the villagers struggled through the brutal winters and the spring would often bring as many funerals as it did flowers. It was for this reason that hasty marriages were common as well, as newly widowed parents would look to find a new partner to care for their grieving children.

In the summer of 1809, John Mills, the town's most prominent farmer, was looking to do just that.

With two daughters at home, both under the age of five, Mr. Mills needed a wife capable of managing the home and willing to do the hard work in the fields until their future sons were old enough to pull their weight.

Mary Grace had a gentle temperament; she was the kind of

girl better suited to living in town and spending her time at church or crafting candles by the fire. The young orphan, by contrast, was accustomed to difficult work, both inside and out of the home. She had spent many summers on the shore gathering clams with her father, and once her mother fell ill, the caretaking had largely fallen to her. She was no stranger to soiled sheets, night terrors, last rites read by dying candlelight, or the raspy gasps of imminent death. John Mills figured that a young woman who had endured such experiences could easily handle two small children and a few farm animals.

Mr. Mills had no problem making the arrangements with Mary Grace's father, who viewed the proposal as a divine stroke of luck for the daughter of a mere fisherman. But unbeknownst to both men, the girls had been keeping a secret.

His name was Michael James, and while the rest of the town seemed not to notice the way he looked at her, Mary Grace could read her best friend like no other. She saw them glance at each other across the pews in church and knew exactly why her friend had recently acquired an interest in cooking fish for dinner every night of the week: Michael worked as a fisherman down at the docks.

And because Mary Grace loved her friend as she would love a sister, both girls were perhaps equally upset by the news her father broke at the supper table that fateful evening.

"Mary Grace will help you pack your clothes," he instructed. "The wedding will take place this Sunday after the services, and Mr. Mills will take you back to the farm."

It was such a simple command; a decision that would forever change her life delivered as though the family had been discussing what to eat for breakfast the next day.

Her heart sank, but alas, she knew better than to refuse.

The service was simple. The bride carried a small bouquet of violets. It wasn't until the reverend pronounced them Man and Wife that she looked at his face and into his eyes. He was nearly twice her age, still handsome, though farm life had aged him beyond his years. His hands were rough and calloused and his shoulders seemed to be in a permanent state of tension due to years of leaning over, tending the earth and milking the cows.

John shook hands with Mary Grace's father. Mary Grace's mother held the bride close, wishing her a lifetime of happiness. As for Mary Grace herself, she quietly mourned the loss of her adopted sister, but said nothing. The two hugged each other tight, and the bride was startled to feel a note slipped into one hand a second before John reached for the other.

As she climbed onto the wagon and sat beside her husband, she saw him: Michael, across the road, gazing at her in a manner so subtle, no one nearby could have seen the hurt in his eyes. No one, at least, but the young bride herself.

* * *

Flora, age four, and Lydia, age three, were well behaved and curious to meet their stepmother. To her relief, they were happy to see their father, who smiled wide and scooped them up into his arms as soon as he opened the door to the farmhouse.

She roasted a chicken for supper, and though she did not have the time to bake a proper loaf of bread, she vowed to do so the following day. The family ate together in relative silence, save for the occasional giggle as one of the children attempted to tickle the other.

This was her life now, and there was nothing to be done but accept it. But her heart ached. The farm was far from town and from the only family she had left. John would leave her alone often because of the endless work to be done in the fields. And Michael...

The thought of losing him hurt most of all. He was young, not yet a man of established means like John, and would therefore not be seen as a suitable husband, but she did not care.

Other than Mary Grace, Michael was the first person to see her beyond her responsibilities. He had first been a friend to her when her mother was ill, often asking not of her mother's condition, but of her own well being. He inquired about her interests and upon discovering her love of mulberries, went out of his way to collect some from a neighbor's property any day he suspected she might come to see him at the market.

Perhaps John was a good man, but this marriage was about duty and sacrifice. It had nothing to do with love.

Night fell. While John tucked the children into their beds, she crept into the bedroom and reached for the note Mary Grace had given her at the church.

Dearest,

My heart breaks to know I could not offer to you the life you have been promised by Mr. Mills. I have taken leave of my work at the docks and will set sail tomorrow morning on a fishing expedition. I would give anything to bring you with me, to sail across the waves all through the day and lay together under the bright stars at night. I could not leave without declaring to you, my darling, my love for you and my regret for failing to become your husband. I wish you happiness at your new home and hope our paths cross again in another life.

With love,
Michael

The click of the door opening startled her and she quickly stuffed the note under the mattress just as John entered the room.

Without looking at her face, he tugged at the laces of her nightgown, slipping it down past her shoulders. She shuddered as a draft stung her bare skin. John put his strong hands on her arms, first seeming to warm her, then gently pushed her back onto the bed.

She looked at the ceiling and tried to relax. He held her for just a minute, then kissed her on the forehead. She closed her eyes.

* * *

John slept soundly beside her, but she was wide-awake, consumed by the thought of Michael setting sail, perhaps, as had been the case with her father, never to return. The unrelenting thoughts finally inspired her to creep quietly out of bed and hastily retrieve her shoes.

The amber sunlight had just begun to kiss the water as she rode up on John's horse. The ship was busy with men loading crates and barrels, preparing for weeks away from home. He was there, among them, moments away from closing up the ship and sailing out to sea.

"Michael!" She shouted, loud enough to get the attention of half a dozen men. He ran to her with a look of grave concern. She dismounted the horse and met his embrace.

"What are you thinking? Are you mad?"

"Don't go. Don't leave me."

"It is too late to abandon my position. I cannot stay."

"I will come with you, then."

"It is too dangerous. Surely, I cannot bring a married woman - or any woman - on an expedition such as this."

"But your letter—"

"I stated the truth of how I feel, not the truth of what is possible."

"Let us run away, then. Any port in the colonies is in constant want of fishermen. We can be together anywhere we please. I love you, Michael."

Michael looked at her face, her skin red from the cold morning air, her eyes shining in the soft light of the sunrise, and frowned.

"It is too late. You have taken your vows and I cannot be the man who breaks the heart of an already grieving family. It would be a sin."

She shook her head. "It cannot be too late! No one in our new village would ever need to know."

"God will know. And, eventually, so will your husband."

He wrapped his arms around her and kissed her on the head.

"I must be going. John Mills is a noble man, and I have no doubt that you will be a wonderful wife to him."

And with that, he turned away from her and hurried back to his shipmates. She watched from the hillside as the ship became smaller, though her longing for him seemed to grow as deep as the ocean itself.

The sun was high and the sky blue when she returned to the farm. She would have to tell John she panicked at the thought of moving away from her best friend and found herself going back for a proper good-bye. Fear gripped her entire body as she wondered if he would believe her story, and if he didn't, what he would say or do to her as punishment. But her only other choice would be to run, and with no money, no food, and nowhere to go, that wasn't a choice at all.

A lump crawled into her throat as she approached the farm. Something was wrong.

Strange horses surrounded the home and a small crowd of neighbors had gathered around a wagon. An older woman sat on the porch with Flora and Lydia in her arms, both of them sobbing uncontrollably.

The icy glares they sent to her confirmed her worst fear: lying in the back of the wagon, wrapped in a sheet from her own marital bed, lay the body of John Mills.

Having found no indications of violence on his body, the town council concluded that John must have been murdered through acts of witchcraft. Her family's fate had long ago aroused suspicion from the rest of the town, and now the adulterous note from Michael found in the bedroom, coupled with her escape and subsequent return to the scene of the crime (proof, in their eyes, of a guilty conscience), led to a singular conclusion on the matter of who must have conspired with the Devil to commit such an act of malice against him.

The rumors were unbearably cruel. Some people in the town swore they had seen her plant poison hemlock in the garden she had so dutifully attended to at Mary Grace's home and brought it with her to the farm with the intention of killing not only her husband, but the children as well. Others insisted a mere kiss from a minion of Satan would suck the life from a man, and that John Mills had unknowingly sealed his own death warrant the moment he had married her.

She would have hung if not for the persistence of Mary Grace's parents. Having given up on convincing the town of their adopted daughter's innocence, they instead pleaded with the council not to allow their town to meet the same fate Salem had a century before. Salem lived on in infamy for the disaster the panic of the witch trials had caused, which in the end had seen hundreds of innocents imprisoned and nineteen of them killed.

No, they insisted, Portland must be better than this. The best way to protect the town from such catastrophe was to allow the accused to live in exile, alone, far from where she could ever harm another soul. Thus, the orphaned girl turned widow was banished from the town of Portland and henceforth referred to only as the Witch.

* * *

The years went by slowly.

The Witch made do with her solitary lifestyle, but the matter of forgiveness was something else entirely. She couldn't be bothered with that blissful, fleeting feeling of denial. She never allowed herself that moment upon waking where one forgets their plight in the faintest hint of the dawn, only to remember and relive the horror over again seconds later. Nor could she wrap herself in the twisted comfort of shock, numbing her nerves to the outside world, her mind ill-equipped to comprehend its own misery. No, she could have none of that. Rather, she seethed in anger in every waking moment, anger that had spread through her entire body as the hateful rumors about her had spread through the town of Portland.

When she toiled away, planting in the garden in the spring, she hated them. When she harvested the berries in the summer and the root vegetables in the autumn, she hated them. She made candles by the fire and hated them. She skinned rabbits, raccoons, and squirrels to sew clothing from their pelts and hated them.

The townspeople feared her, but in need of an honest living, the Witch resolved to swallow her rage when one might be occasionally desperate enough to make the two-hour journey to the cottage for her help.

The Witch had cultivated a large herb garden and studied the various effects an herbal concoction could have on one's mind and body. It was a twisted way in which she had become what they expected her to be, as it was common knowledge that the medicinal properties one could find in nature was something only a witch could fully understand.

This was, in fact, how the Witch had learned that Mary Grace had married a few years later. A handsome young blacksmith by the name of Alexander Roth had paid the Witch a visit, asking for anything to lesson the pain of a lost pregnancy. Her heart broke for her estranged sister, but she felt an overwhelming sense of relief knowing Mary Grace had a husband who cared for her enough to make such a journey at the risk of damaging his own reputation. Neither he nor Mary Grace had returned since, and the Witch spent many an hour wondering if they had been able to have another baby.

The Witch also made a modest living by allowing weary travelers to spend the night in her cottage. The home rested on a small hill and could be seen from the main road leading to Portland, and even though Portland was just two more hours away, many travelers riding into the night could not resist the call of a warm bed and a homemade stew, and figured whatever business needed to be accomplished in town would best be done after a good night's rest.

The Witch would provide just that. Sacrificing her own bed and sharing her dinner, she would instead stay awake all night in her rocking chair by the fire, sewing or perhaps bundling dried herbs with a knife at her waist, just in case.

* * *

Five winters had passed since her banishment and a sixth was forthcoming.

It was a peaceful autumn morning when the Witch ventured into the woods, as she did every morning, to retrieve any small animals that had found themselves trapped in a deep hole she had dug in the ground and lightly covered with twigs and leaves. The ground was frosty and the air was thick, signaling the impending arrival of the first snow of the season.

It was a disappointment to see that one trap had clearly been stepped in, but the creature had managed to escape. It happened from time to time. She reset the twigs and shook her head. It must have been a large one - a rabbit, perhaps - to have jumped out of a hole so deep, and thus, would have made a stew that could have lasted for days.

She made her way to the carrot patch and found many of them gone. This was a bit stranger, as they had clearly not been dug from the dirt, but rather plucked.

Surrounded by so much silence, the Witch would occasionally find herself haunted by the feeling that someone, most likely a townsperson seeking retribution, could be watching her, and the thought of it caused the ever-present sense of rage to force its way into her chest.

A feeling of warmth collected in her fingertips as she pulled in a deep breath. She paused for a moment in the stillness of the woods, a space so intimately familiar to her she knew its every movement. A light breeze caused a few red leaves to fall to the ground. It was quiet, but something was different.

Placing a hand on the knife at her belt, she spun around to the trees behind her.

"Who goes there?"

There was no answer. She stepped closer.

"I know you are hiding. Reveal yourself now and be done with it."

A figure slowly emerged from the heavy brush. It was a horse.

She lowered her knife and stared at the creature, puzzled. The horse was in fine shape. It had clearly been fed and even had a rope hastily fashioned around its neck to resemble reins. She mounted the horse with the largest jump she could muster - an awkward one at that, given the size of the animal - grabbed it by the mane, and held the knife to its throat.

"Come out now or I shall turn your horse into a meal large enough to last through winter!"

Finally, a man appeared from behind a large bush.

"My apologies," said a deep but quivering voice. "I mean you no harm. I just needed a place to rest and something to eat. Please do not hurt the animal. I need him. I have a long journey ahead."

She took in the sight before her. He was young and healthy by all appearances, save for the pale skin that indicated he had not eaten much lately. Finally, she noticed his attire: a military uniform.

"You are a Navy man?"

"Yes."

"You seem to be far from home, sailor."

"You do not know the half of it, I'm afraid."

"Are you lost?"

"In a manner of speaking, yes, I am."

She straightened up on the horse, indignant. "Did you take an animal from a trap this morning?"

He took a few steps back and reached behind a tree, retrieving a large rabbit with a broken neck.

"Please believe me, I do not wish to steal from you, but it has been two days since I last ate and I am desperate for food."

The Witch was unsure of what to do with this man. She thought of all the uses she could have for the horse. Not to eat, that was a hollow threat she had posed to the stranger in the bushes; but with a horse, she could venture far into the woods to collect as many herbs and berries as she could find. She could plant potatoes and carrots anywhere she found the best soil and carry loads of them back to her cottage. Yes, she needed the horse, and the man needed to find his ship.

"I propose a trade," she finally said to him. "I will take you where you need to go, and once you have arrived, I will return home with your horse."

"With respect, my lady, I do not believe that is a good idea."

"Alternatively, I can ride into town right at this moment and alert the authorities as to your whereabouts. I am certain they can reunite you with your men."

"It is not that simple. There has been a battle about two days north of here. Many of my men have been scattered throughout the region, and I fear it will take a great amount of effort to find and reunite those of us lucky enough to still be alive." He looked up at her with a tired resignation. "I beg of you, just let me be on my way. You may have the rabbit and we shall never see each other again."

Perhaps it was because the Witch knew the pain of a life removed from one's home, or perhaps it was simply because it had been months since she had set eyes on another human being, but whatever the reason, the Witch observed his pitiful offering of a dead rabbit in exchange for his freedom and decided the matter would be best discussed over a warm bowl of rabbit stew.

* * *

He ate so quickly she worried he would choke. She took her time, partially to savor the fresh stew and the almost-stale bread she had leftover from the day before, but mostly to watch him.

"What is your name, sailor?"

He looked up with a smirk. "Forgive me, in all the excitement I have clearly forgotten all of my manners. Petty Officer Isaac H. Perry."

"And how did you come to be separated from your men, Officer Petty?"

He chuckled and cleared his throat. "Perry," he politely corrected.

She smiled and blushed a little. "Pardon me. Officer Perry."

The smile faded from his face as he prepared a response to her question. "Are you aware of what's happening on the shores right now? The conflict with the British?"

She shook her head.

"The Redcoats have arrived, again. We met them at the wharf near Hampden with a large number of men, but their reinforcements proved to be too much for us. The battle descended into chaos, and I... I eventually came to, alone in the woods."

She glanced at the window and saw the color of the world had shifted to a dark grey as the clouds surrounded them. The first storm of the season was usually followed by sunnier days before the winter settled in to stay for a number of months. Perhaps tomorrow, even, the sun would be out and his risk of freezing on his journey through the woods would be substantially lower.

"You may stay here tonight, if you wish," she told him.

"I could not impose on you---"

She held up her hand, uninterested in his polite objection that ultimately amounted to no more than an empty platitude.

"The woods here are dangerous. It is not wise to brave them in the snow."

"Thank you. You are a very generous woman."

Generous was one of the few descriptors the Witch had never heard directed toward her.

He slept through most of the afternoon, which worried her a little; if he were to be up all night, she would need to be especially careful to stay up as well. Trust was something the Witch had long since given up finding with others.

The snow began to fall just as the sun disappeared behind the ridge. The Witch stepped outside, wrapped in a fur blanket, and drank a tea made from birch and elderberry. She met the horse's gaze for a moment, then approached him, placing her fur blanket on his back and stroking him softly on the nose. He blinked at her. She suspected the horse was as grateful for a place to rest as was his master.

Given Mr. Perry's ordeal in the war, she expected him to stir in his sleep, but exhaustion had clearly taken its toll. He was so still she crept up to him and watched carefully to ensure he was breathing.

He finally roused himself from her bed just before supper, the smell of fresh bread and fried potatoes no doubt tempting him back from even the deepest slumber. He took in his surroundings and noted the snow on the windowsill.

"You were right, I should not be riding in this storm."

The Witch did not respond. She knew she had been right.

Without a word, she handed him a plate of food, which he ate quickly despite his efforts to pace himself.

"You are too kind to me. I find myself in disbelief that I could have stumbled upon someone so lovely during this godforsaken war."

Though she was always wary of compliments from strangers, she couldn't help but feel happy hearing one after so much time spent in isolation.

"So, I have told you my story," said Mr. Perry. "Now tell me yours."

She shrugged. "There is little to tell. I enjoy the quiet beauty of the woods."

"Forgive my saying so, but it seems as though a beautiful woman such as yourself would have no trouble finding a husband."

"I had a husband, for a short time," she said, neglecting to mention just how short the time had been. "Losing him...was a painful ordeal that I would prefer not to experience again."

She left her explanation vague, knowing he would assume she had had a difficult mourning period, when in truth, she had never grieved for John; the painful ordeal to which she referred was an entirely different form of grief.

"I see," he stated, though he clearly couldn't have understood what she really meant. "But you must be lonely out here."

"I have found that loneliness is a part of all of us, no matter how many people we have nearby. Did you ever feel lonely in the Navy?"

"Of course."

"Even surrounded by the rest of your men?"

"I take your point."

The room fell silent and the Witch struggled with what to say next. She had cultivated many strengths after several years in the woods, but conversation was not one of them. She couldn't help but notice the way the fire sparkled in his brown eyes. For a brief moment, she thought of Michael.

*   *   *

That night, the Witch dreamt of John and the way he touched her on her first and only night at the farmhouse. She closed her eyes as he climbed on top of her, but seconds later, opened them and found herself alone and naked in an open field. Suddenly, the air filled with the loud boom of a cannon, the heavy thud of bodies slamming into the ground, and the screams of terrified men. She wrapped her arms around herself, shivering in the cold night air, and searched the woods for the source of the noise, but could see nothing.

She woke to find herself in her rocking chair. She had fallen asleep despite her best efforts to stay awake and keep watch over the stranger in her bed. She reached for the knife in her belt, but quickly realized he was sound asleep again and posed no threat to her.

The snow continued well into the morning. The Witch had hoped that the sun would return and melt enough of the snow to make the journey safe for him, but it now seemed that the storm would continue throughout the day and possibly into the night again. There was little for either of them to do but wait.

"Do you like music?" he asked her, breaking a long period of silence.

"Of course."

"As a child I wanted to become a reverend, though not because I had any interest in providing spiritual guidance to anyone. I prefer to keep my faith to myself, to be blunt. Still, the reverends were allowed to sing and to play the organ. It was the highlight of every week for me, singing in church."

"I do not have an organ for you here, I'm afraid," she teased. "But I would like it if you sang your favorite hymn."

He gave a sly smile. "I thought you liked the quiet."

"Mostly, but it is so rare I have company, especially someone with any musical talent. Indulge me."

Suddenly shy, he gathered his nerve and began to sing, softly at first before finally finding his confidence.

> *"Lo, how a rose e'er blooming*
> *From tender stem hath sprung,*
> *Of Jesse's lineage coming*
> *As men of old have sung*
> *It came a flower bright,*
> *Amid the cold of winter*
> *When half spent was the night."*

"That's lovely. I do not believe I have heard it before."

"It's a popular tune where I come from."

"Where is that?"

He paused briefly, taking bite of leftover bread. "Near

Providence. Have you ever been to that region?"

"I have never been outside of this region."

"The summers are lovely there. Of course I imagine the summers are lovely just about anywhere."

There was another silence as the conversation came to a natural pause.

"The snow will continue for awhile. The day is still young," she said, picking up another fur blanket from beside the fire and wrapping it around her shoulders. "Tell me what happened up north. I know you are not seeking to be reunited with your men, or you would not be rushing so far south so quickly."

His demeanor darkened. The lighthearted joy she had just begun to see in him once he sang his favorite hymn and spoke of his home had faded away.

"This would not be a polite conversation for a lady."

"I am no lady," she said, almost with a slight chuckle. "Haven't you realized by now? I am out here in the woods all alone. I am a witch."

Now it was his turn to hold back a chuckle. "Are you now?"

She finally allowed herself to laugh, just a little. "That is what they say."

"People say a great many things that are not true, especially in towns such as this. The larger cities pay little attention to such superstitions as you find in the smaller villages."

He did not believe her. It was a surprise and an enormous sense of relief. Isaac must have been the first man ever to cross her path without fear. Even those who paid her for a bed for the night en route to Portland seemed to eye her with suspicion, and of course, anyone from town knew to stay far away from her lest they meet the same fate John Mills had those years ago.

"Why do they call you a witch?"

She longed to tell him more of her story, especially once the realization came that she had never spoken of it to anyone. Her banishment had happened so quickly, she had not even had time to speak of it with Mary Grace. Long weeks in her prison cell during the trial had been swiftly replaced with long weeks at her cottage without a moment between, and the rare travelers who spent the night with her were not an appropriate audience.

And now, here was Isaac, a man who was hardly in a position to judge her for her alleged indiscretions. As soon as the storm passed, he would be on his way home, and the two would never see each other again. Surely, it must be safe to tell him, for he could never reveal her secrets to anyone without revealing his own.

"They believe I killed my husband."

"Did you?" He asked, already knowing the answer.

"No."

The Witch declined to elaborate at that moment, instead waiting on Isaac to speak. He steeled himself in preparation for his tale.

"Bangor has been ransacked and nearly burned to the ground by the Redcoats. I was optimistic at the start of this war, as we have defeated the British army before, and with fewer men than we have now at the ready. But this man, this Captain Barrie, he is a complete lunatic. He spared the lives of all who lived in town, thank Heaven for that, but little else. His men killed livestock, destroyed furniture, and set much of the town to burn, including ships in the harbor. I had..."

He paused for a moment and reached for a small basin of water, helping himself to a drink. "I had recently received word from Providence that my mother had fallen ill. I am now an only child, as my brother Thomas succumbed to influenza when we were children and my sister Emily did not survive infancy. When I saw the devastation in Bangor, I knew I was beyond my depth. I could not help these people, no matter how much I wished to. But my mother needed me, and I felt compelled to go to her, as if driven by a force much larger than myself. The path into the woods was so clear; the horse was right there and available to me. I took it as a sign from God, thanked Him for my survival, and left."

The Witch did not say anything, nor did she look away.

"I am a deserter and a traitor to my country. Should I be discovered here, I shall be tried and imprisoned, perhaps killed. I am putting you in danger by being here due to my own selfishness. I came upon your home cold, hungry, and desperate, and failing to act as a man of integrity, I put my needs ahead of yours. Now you have been nothing but kind to me and I regret my actions deeply. Please, you must know how sorry I am to have forced the consequences of my decisions upon you."

It may have been the first time she had ever heard a man

express such regret, save for the ill-fated love letter from Michael.

"Well, fortunately for both of us, your horse is out back and not visible from the main road. It is unlikely anyone will see him. In fact, in this storm, it is unlikely anyone will see the road itself. For now, it seems we are safe."

* * *

The snow stopped shortly before nightfall. The Witch decided to go out to retrieve more firewood, though first had great difficulty opening the door against the packed, icy snow that had nearly sealed it to the ground.

Her boots were old and falling apart. Though she had been able to sew plenty of skirts and shawls for herself out of small animal pelts, the procurement of leather and fastening it in the shape of boots was not a skill she possessed, and her feet were cold as they crunched through the snow around the cottage.

An axe lay next to a pile of wood that had mostly kept dry underneath an overhang out back. She set a small log in position to be chopped and was about to raise the axe when Isaac's voice stopped her.

"Allow me," he said behind her. He took the axe from her and swung at the log, splitting it in two.

With Isaac helping, she was free to check a few of her traps, though she had to dig through the snow that had filled every hole in the ground with her bare hands. A rabbit and a squirrel lay frozen inside one of them, and for a moment she pitied the poor creatures. They typically weren't in there for long before she would find them and swiftly break their necks, allowing for a quick and nearly painless death. These two must have frozen to death under the snow, and may have also been on the brink of starvation.

It didn't matter now. She brought both back to the cottage and set them near the fire to thaw before skinning them and adding them to the stew pot for supper.

The fire was nearly dead. She glanced over her shoulder to be sure Isaac's attention was directed elsewhere, then gingerly cupped her hands over the remaining embers. She rocked her hands back and forth and the embers slowly grew into flames.

Isaac came through the door behind her, firewood in hand. "Whatever would I have done in this storm had I not been fortunate enough to find this place? I'd be asleep in the snow somewhere, freezing and starving. I suppose my actions could be construed as a dramatic escape or a fool's errand."

She laughed and realized this was the most relaxed she had been in quite some time. Living in exile meant there was always a faint fear in her mind that someone unwelcome would come to her door: a traveler at best, and at worst, an angry villager poised to accuse her of some other wrongdoing. Or, in the best possible scenario, she dreamed that one day Mary Grace would come back for her, children in hand, and tell her none of it mattered now; the town had forgotten all about John Mills and she would be free to join their family again. Perhaps, even, that Michael had finally come back from the sea.

None of these things weighed on her mind now that Isaac was here. His presence made her feel safe in a way she could not explain, for he was still a relative stranger. Along with the heat from the fire, a new kind of warmth began to burn in her chest.

"I hope you will not find me too immodest," she said. He perked up and looked at her with an expression she could only identify as hope. "But I must remove these wet boots."

"Of course, this is your home after all. In fact, would you prefer I step out for a minute? You must not have changed your clothes since I have been here."

That was true, and perhaps it would have been a good idea for him to do just that, but she didn't want him to leave. "No, please stay. It's perfectly all right, I just need to warm my feet and allow them to dry."

She removed the boots and Isaac swiftly picked one up.

"This is what you have been wearing every day?"

"I am not a very skilled cobbler, I'm afraid."

"Well, neither am I, but certainly we can do better than this."

He leaned over to reach for her sewing supplies in their basket by the fire, and in doing so, brought his face within inches of hers, nearly bumping her head with his.

He laughed, awkwardly. "Excuse me, I apologize for that."

"No need," she said with a smile.

Their eyes met. In a moment of pure instinct, without thinking, she touched his hair and kissed him gently.

* * *

The rest of the evening was extraordinary.

She had never been touched this way by a man other than John Mills, which was to say she had never been touched this way by a man she wanted to have. It was electrifying and romantic. Suddenly, she realized her greatest gift in being separated from the rest of the people of Portland: she may have been shunned from their lives, but that also meant she was free of their rules. No reverend could chastise her for something he knew nothing of, for no one was around to tell him. Isaac would leave in the morning and their night spent together would be a secret she would keep forever.

Furthermore, if they already believed she was destined to eternal damnation, either for killing John Mills (which she hadn't) or for leaving him to engage in an early morning rendezvous with Michael (which she had), then the added sin of sexual relations outside marriage meant nothing more to God or to the Devil. But here on Earth, it meant everything to her.

They slept peacefully together, tightly wound in each other's arms, when she felt Isaac jolt in his sleep and gasp for air. She sprang up and looked toward the door, expecting an intruder, but found the home empty.

Isaac thrashed again in the bed, and she realized this was what she had expected when he first arrived: night terrors, similar to the ones her mother had had when she was a child. Those who had seen death in their mind's eye could not stop seeing it, especially in dreams. She tightly gripped his bare shoulder and shook him.

"Isaac, wake up. Wake up."

His eyes finally opened.

"You are safe. You are here with me."

It took him a moment to remember his surroundings and even remember her face, but once he did, he breathed a huge sigh of relief and laid his head back on her pillow.

"Thank the Lord," was all he could say.

She draped a blanket over her naked body and moved to the fireplace, adding her iron kettle above the fire. Moments later, she brought him a warm cup of tea from her collection of dried herbs.

"Peppermint. It will help you find a more restful sleep."

He smiled at her as he drank the tea. "You may not be a witch," he said, gently touching her hair. "But to me, you are magic."

*   *   *

The Witch had woken up angry every morning for more than five years, but not today. Today dawned with a glowing sensation of happiness, followed immediately by a sense of sorrow. Isaac would need to leave today. The storm had passed and it was best for him to continue on his journey before anyone discovered him here. She thought of this as she ate slightly toasted bread for breakfast and gazed out the window.

Isaac rolled over in the bed and reached for her, then opened his eyes when he realized she wasn't there.

"You're up," was all he could manage to say in his sleepy state as he spotted her silhouette against the window.

"The sun is, as well. I suppose you had better be going to make the most of the day on your travels."

He wrapped a blanket around himself as he stood and crossed to the window beside her.

"I was thinking...if the sun is out all day, perhaps it will melt more of the snow and make the journey easier tomorrow. Meanwhile, I could fix your boots and the crack in the wall here, where a lot of cold air is coming through."

He gestured to a gap between the stone wall and the roof near the front door. "And if you have the pelts to spare, perhaps you could make something for me to help keep warm. A small blanket, or even just a hat."

He wanted to stay. She felt her ribcage gripped with anxiety, but her excitement overpowered her fear. The chores he proposed could all be completed eventually, but now, in the cold early morning, they found their way back to bed.

One day became two. Two days became three. Her boots were mended, the crack under the ceiling had been repaired with mud, and she had made for him several bags of herbal teas, gloves, a pair of socks, and bundles of carrots for the horse.

Wrapped in a blanket by the fire that evening, she tried not to think about his inevitable departure. No matter how many reasons they found for him to stay, the fact remained that he had a family to care for, and his presence at her home would not be safe for either of them.

It did not surprise her when he said, "There is something I must tell you." Expecting him to pack up and finally be on his way in the morning, she readied herself to say good-bye.

She was not prepared for what he said next. "I have not been entirely truthful with you. My mother is not ill, and I am not from Providence. The truth is, I am from a small village on the Bay of Fundy. Do you know where that is?"

She shook her head.

"It is north of Bangor. Quite north, in fact. Beyond the border of Maine."

She took a moment to consider the depth of what he was saying. "You fought for the British, then?" She sent a glance to the Navy coat resting on the back of her rocking chair.

"I took the coat from a wounded sailor on the battlefield."

"Why would you tell me otherwise?"

"You are an American, are you not? I was afraid that anyone I encountered on my journey south would shoot me dead at first sight, which is why I stole the coat."

"Why journey south at all, if not for a family who needs you? For that matter, why run if you and your men had won the battle?"

He looked into the fire and sighed heavily. "You must understand, I never wanted to be a seaman. Not for a moment in my entire life. I was just a boy of fourteen when I was taken. I had just begun work as a logger, the youngest on my crew. The older men went to the pub after a particularly long day and invited me to come along. I craved their approval desperately and I am afraid I overdid it with the whiskey that night. I fell asleep on a table and when I woke, my crew had all gone home, leaving me there alone."

The cottage seemed to grow darker around her, save for the glow of the fire on the side of Isaac's face. As he spoke, he could not bring himself to look at her eyes.

"I stumbled out of the tavern, dizzy and with a burning thirst in my throat. A nice man passed by and offered me water. I drank the contents of the canteen in seconds and he offered more if I were to come back to his ship. I declined, figuring it were best that I find my way home, when I felt the sharpest pain I had ever experienced in my life. Another man had struck me on the back of the head with a club, and without warning, several men were beating me on the ground - I could not even discern how many there were. I was carried to the ship and spent the night below deck with a handful of other young men in a similar state as myself. The next morning, the ship had set sail, and from that moment on, I found myself a member of the Royal Navy."

The Witch was unsure of what to do in light of this revelation. She felt she should be outraged at the thought of harboring a member of an enemy army in her home. Then again, the rules of American society did not necessarily apply in this situation. But there was also a matter of trust. He had lied to her not once, but twice now about his identity and reason for his escape. She wondered if there was any reason to believe him now.

"As I have told you," he continued, "I was a sensitive boy who loved to play with my younger brother and sing in church on Sundays. My parents were gentle people who never so much as spoke an unkind word to anyone in our village. I was, and still am, a pacifist. I do not, nor would I ever, wish the terrors of war on my worst enemy. When Captain Barrie commanded the sacking of Bangor and Hampden, I had had enough. I was in America, and vowed to stay. After grabbing the horse and procuring an American military coat, I rode south with no destination in mind, just a desire to go as far as possible from the madness I had witnessed. Perhaps I will make it to New York or even to Washington. I intend to start over and make my way as best I can. I am not afraid of hard work or manual labor, and I must trust that this will be enough to survive in America."

Her head grew heavy. She strongly empathized with him, since she herself had narrowly escaped an onslaught of brutality after her husband's passing and knew the sensation of pure and unabashed fear of a violent death. And to have witnessed so much destruction against his will and indeed against his very nature must have been horrifying.

She also felt afraid. The lingering anxiety that had plagued her over the years of the threat of an unwelcome visitor was heightened to the point of near panic now. He needed to run.

"Say something," he pleaded, and it occurred to her that for all the thoughts swimming in her mind, she had remained silent.

"Isaac, I..." *I want you to leave*, she thought. *I need you to go far away for your own safety.* "I want you to stay."

She hadn't expected the words to come out of her mouth, but there they were, hanging thick in the air between them. She was overcome with a feeling stronger than any she had felt before, even for Michael. Looking at Isaac made her heart beat stronger and her blood run warmer.

This was not a simple infatuation. This was love.

"Run away with me," he said with a searing optimism in his voice. "There is no reason for you to stay. We can begin again. A new town, a fresh start for both of us. We can be married, perhaps even raise a family."

The Witch had long since given up on the idea of marriage and motherhood, but now, the thought excited her. A whole new life flashed before her eyes: she and Isaac living in a New York row home, with enough of a yard for her garden and within a reasonable distance from growing businesses in need of eager young workers. Or perhaps a small house farther south in Virginia, where the weather was warmer, the soil was softer, and green, grassy meadows could be filled with the sound of a child's laughter.

She looked at him and saw their future in his eyes, and simply said, "Yes."

* * *

The Witch had a very small amount of money; not enough to rent a home, but perhaps just enough for a night at an inn should the weather take a turn for the worse. Hopefully, the temperature would cooperate and remain warm enough for them to sleep outside near a fire. If that were the case, and if she were able to trap and cook rabbits along the way, they could make it as far as New York in as little as four days and sell the horse to quickly raise enough money for food and shelter while Isaac began to look for work.

The very idea of it thrilled her. A man from New York had stayed at the cottage two years prior, and compared to the other tenants she had put up for a night at a time, this one was particularly talkative - and, perhaps, particularly homesick. He spoke of how quickly the city was changing, with new roads stretching on for miles, bustling streets, expansive rivers, and new opportunities growing by the day. It was a settlement that longed to be as big as London, and in his opinion, would be within the next several years.

Her childhood dreams of discovering an exotic new land flooded back into her mind. Though the crowded city streets overwhelmed her in a sense, the thought also, paradoxically, made her feel safe. She would need not worry about exposure in a place where one could so easily be lost in the daily hustle and bustle. In the woods of Maine, they were outsiders, forever branded with a target on their backs. In the city of New York, they would simply be a married couple, going about their lives and minding their own business. After five years alone, the thought suited her just fine.

Besides, they were prepared to start over now, and if they found the city did not suit them after all, they could do it again.

She woke the second the sun's first ray crept onto the windowsill. The fire had gone out during the night and the stone cottage was cold - so cold she could see a faint trace of her breath in the air.

But it wasn't just the frigid autumn morning that made the room cold. She had a sinking feeling in her gut. Something was wrong.

She quickly rolled over and a flash of fear overcame her. Was she afraid for Isaac? Was he all right? She suddenly thought of John Mills' body laying still in the back of the cart on that terrible day.

"Isaac, wake up," she said with more haste and concern in her voice than she had intended. He stirred and opened his eyes; she exhaled a sigh of relief.

"What is the matter?" He asked.

"I am not sure." She kissed the side of his head. "Come. We must be going. We may be able to make it as far as Massachusetts today if we leave right away."

It took them seconds to get ready, dressing in furs and carrying as much food as they could in small satchels. For a moment she considered saying a prayer, or at least taking a silent moment alone to say good-bye to the stone cottage that had housed and protected her through these difficult years, but something in the back of her mind told her there was no time. They needed to go.

Bundled in fur and about to step into the sunlight, she expected the chill in the back of her spine to subside. Instead, the moment they opened the door, the feeling deepened, seeping under her skin and into her blood. Men in red coats, armed, with their horses standing dutifully nearby, surrounded the cottage.

"Good morning, Mr. Perry," a man said. The words were simultaneously spoken with a dignified accent and a sinister hiss.

Isaac froze beside her.

"Mr. Perry, I would think by now you should be aware of how

one must properly address a superior. Has your time away from your post affected your memory, or shall I interpret your silence as an act of disrespect?"

Isaac stood up as straight as a board. "Aye aye, sir. Good day, Captain."

"Good morning, Miss," the man said to her. "Are you aware you have been harboring a fugitive of the British Royal Navy?" She wanted to respond, but felt as though her throat had frozen.

"No, sir. As you may observe," Isaac interjected, gesturing to his blue coat, "she had not the faintest idea of my true identity."

The Captain made a *tisk* sound as he shook his head. "It is a sin to lie, Seaman - and to such a lovely young lady, too. Although, perhaps she has kept a secret or two from you as well? The fine townspeople of Portland have many opinions as to her integrity."

Her heart dropped from her chest so heavily she winced in pain. *They* had done this. How they knew, she could not decipher for sure, but she recalled the frequent feelings of unease that came over her from time to time, all alone in the cottage, half expecting an unwelcome guest from town. Perhaps someone had been there all along, surveying her and waiting to catch her in an act of indiscretion. It would not have been difficult to discern Isaac's identity, as Bangor was not terribly far away, and news of the battle surely would have reached Portland shortly afterwards. When men in red coats came looking for a missing seaman, the townspeople would have had no qualms about turning him in, especially if it implicated the infamous, murderous Witch in the process.

The Captain looked around and took a deep, satisfying breath. "I must say, it certainly is lovely out here in the country, is it not? The longer I stand here, the lighter I feel my mood becoming. Because I am of a happier disposition this morning, I will offer you a choice, Mr. Perry: you may return with us to the ship and face court marshal for desertion, in which case you will be hung once you are surely found to be guilty, or," he grabbed a pistol from his belt and pointed it directly at Isaac. "We can hold an informal trial here and you may face a much easier execution."

The Witch grabbed tightly onto Isaac's arm.

"Personally," the Captain continued, "I would prefer the ship, as I would relish the opportunity to set an example for the rest of the men, lest they get any ideas put into their heads by your act of extreme cowardice. On the other hand, we will have to feed you on the journey back - barely enough to keep you alive, of course - and trials are so terribly boring. And I do believe that bringing your head with us to the ship would still prove to be quite an effective deterrent."

"No," she muttered, involuntarily. It was the only word that could be forced from her throat. No, this could not be happening to him, the kindest man she had ever known. No, she could not have come this close to leaving her solitary life behind, only to see it ripped from her fingertips now. No, no, no.

"Please, Sir," Isaac stammered, "I have proved to be a terrible soldier and she has done nothing wrong. Allow us to be on our way. We do not have much to offer, but can pay you for your cooperation."

"Groveling is a pathetic look for a man, Mr. Perry," the Captain said with a look of disgust, "as is such a sad attempt at bribery. But if you will not decide your own fate, as any respectable man surely could, I shall discern from your remarks that you do not wish to leave this land. And so, you never will."

He aimed his pistol at Isaac and fired. Isaac ducked, covering and protecting her as they both fell to their knees.

The Captain prepared to fire again when the Witch locked eyes with him. On her hands and knees, she glared at him with pure hatred. She gripped the earth, raised one hand and balled it into a fist, and slammed it as hard as she could onto the ground. The Captain lurched backwards, knocked off his feet as though he had been tackled.

Every man around them drew his weapon, startled by the force that had come from nowhere. Isaac staggered to his feet, pushing her out of the way as hard as he could. She landed with a thud in the middle of her garden, slush splashing all around her. She spun around to face the rest of his men, but it was too late. Shots echoed through the forest, and in a split second, Isaac's body fell to the ground.

The men calmly and quietly shouldered their muskets and moved back toward their horses. She looked at Isaac, limp and lifeless in the dirt. She knew before she touched him that he was gone. His was the unholy posture of death, limbs weak and stretched out beside him, his face already colorless and cold.

And then it came. From deep within her, beneath her heart and way down into the depths of her soul, a scream emerged.

It was a scream so loud it shook the trees down to their roots. The shutters on the cottage slammed and splintered. The men in red coats dropped to their knees and covered their ears, crying out in pain, although none could be heard over the sound coming from the Witch. The scream stretched on and on, for this was a breath she had been holding inside for years.

Finally, when she stopped to breathe, she stood up and raised her foot, stomping on the ground with a force so powerful, the men were knocked backwards, some tumbling down the hill and into the road. She opened her eyes wide. To their horror, the men saw the grey color fade away as her eyes turned to the darkest shade of black they had ever seen.

She thrust both her hands out in front of her body, and from meters away, hit the Captain with a force of energy so hard it cracked his skull.

She moved onto the other men, one at a time: twisting their necks until they snapped like a chicken's, crushing their ribs as though they were having the life choked out of them by a giant snake, and hurling them backwards into the trunks of the heaviest trees.

She collapsed to her knees and surveyed the scene. Their bodies lay on the cold, hard ground, their faces frozen in twisted expressions of terror.

She wept as she cradled Isaac's lifeless body in her hands. He looked so innocent, younger than his years even, as he lay still and motionless in his stolen blue coat, which now appeared to be too large for his frame.

The forest was silent.

She was alone again.

*   *   *

Hours passed. Her tears had long since dried as she sat in the dirt. The faint smell of rosemary from the garden provided a soft comfort. She found enough strength to stand and to slowly drag Isaac's body into the garden, placing him near the rose bushes. His body would likely remain frozen for most of the winter, but in the spring, he would slowly slip into the soft earth beneath the melting snow, and what was left of him would be covered in roses.

She walked up to the horse and fed him a carrot from her bag before mounting him and riding toward the town, away from the setting sun and into the dark, cold horizon of the village by the sea.

Shopkeepers began to close their shutters for the evening. Wives walked to their homes with armfuls of bread and meat for supper. One by one, as if startled by a draft in an old house, they turned and saw her, pausing whatever tasks they had been rushing to accomplish.

The Witch took slow steps forward, breathing through her nose like a bull, and stomped her foot again, sending shockwaves through the ground as though an earthquake had struck.

There were a few gasps as they all tried to maintain their balance. She stomped again, and again until panic began to set in among them. Finally, she locked her eyes on the church, the site where she had married John Mills and shared her secret, loving glances with Michael all those years ago. In one jerking motion, she shoved her palms out in front of her. A ball of fire erupted through the roof.

She could hear their cries all around her.

"Witch!"

"The Devil has come for us!"

"God, help us!"

"Lord, hear our prayers!"

She set her sights on the villagers running for their lives. They began to lose control of their own legs, running at a pace so powerful their bones began to crack and they fell hard into the ground, smashing their heads upon impact.

A man ran toward her, holding a wooden cross in front of him.

"In the name of the Lord, I cast you back to Hell from whence you have come! Be gone, Devil!" He shouted at her, before the cross was shoved back toward him so forcefully it impaled his throat.

And here it came again: the scream. This time it was a scream not of anguish, but of pure and unadulterated rage. She screamed so hard and loud, her feet began to levitate off the ground. The winds whipped through the street, dust, leaves, and rocks swirling in the air around her. The sea began to roar and waves came crashing down on the docks, washing away the dock workers unfortunate enough to have been out preparing for the next day's excursions. The sun had set behind the ridge, but her body felt hot, as though a fire burned inside her and raged through her veins, pulsing out of her eyes and fingertips.

The fire at the church had spread to structures nearby. Support beams in several buildings suddenly snapped, causing roofs to collapse. Those lucky enough to still be alive tried desperately to crawl away from the flames and protect their fragile bodies from the debris flying through the air.

The screaming stopped. The Witch's feet returned to the earth. Slight hints of grey returned to her eyes, and in her last moments of appreciation for the chaos before her, a small voice spoke up behind her.

"Anna," the familiar voice said.

Tears filled her eyes, as she knew whom she would face as she slowly turned to look behind her.

Mary Grace was with child, but would not be for much longer. She was overcome with emotions and wanted more than anything to thank her long-lost adopted sister for the pain relief she had provided during that horrible lost pregnancy, to tell her of her husband and child back home, and that her second was due to arrive in weeks. She longed to tell her she was sorry for never braving the journey to visit and for standing by helplessly as the town council had sentenced her to a life she never deserved for a crime she had not committed.

But in that terrifying moment, all she could manage was a simple plea. "Please, Anna. Please stop."

*   *   *

Mary Grace Roth enjoyed being a mother. Her daughter, Elizabeth, was now old enough to hold a spoon and play alone in the yard, but young enough to want her mother to hold to her and tell her stories at bedtime. Her son, Matthew, was learning to crawl. Alexander had proven himself to be a suitable husband who worked hard and cared deeply about seeing his wife happy and his children fed and clothed. Their life together had been simple, but Mary Grace never felt anything but content in their home.

Anna was never far from her mind, though in truth, such had been the case long before the incident. It had been true since the day her father announced his arrangement with John Mills. She wondered what would have happened had she not given her the letter from Michael, or better yet, if she had persuaded her father to consider Michael as a suitor before John Mills found himself in need of a young bride.

Whatever may have been, there was nothing to do now but pray for Anna's safety and try to rebuild the town of Portland with a dim and perhaps vain hope that the townspeople would learn a valuable lesson.

Some said they saw her throw herself into the sea in despair. Others speculated that she had retreated back to the woods and had undoubtedly frozen to death as winter set in. Those in town most prone to be convinced of superstitions said she still roamed the street and swore they had heard her screams in the winds at night.

Mary Grace knew all of this to be foolishness and nothing more. Though it pained her to witness the story of her best friend becoming a cautionary folktale, one that would soon be used to frighten children into coming home before dark and behaving themselves in church, the real story of what had happened to the Witch was one Mary Grace would keep to herself, declining to share it with those who were unwilling to hear it.

She longed to believe her friend had settled in a new town, married, and spent her days peacefully tending to her garden. Or perhaps she had found a job as a seamstress or a governess for a well-to-do family with a brood of spoiled children. Or had continued to help other expectant mothers by becoming a midwife.

Wherever she was, Mary Grace had a subtle feeling that her friend would be all right. The village would forever refer to her as The Witch, but the outside world could simply know her as Anna.

The Debutante

New Orleans, LA

1835

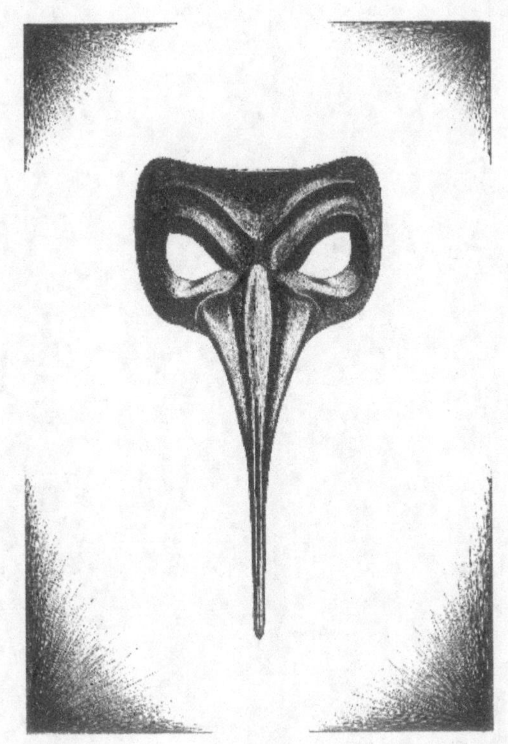

Violet Davenport loved New Orleans, and soon enough, New Orleans would love her right back. She was sixteen now and just two days away from her debut into society, which would take place during the Mardi Gras carnival - the most exciting time of the year, in Violet's humble opinion.

Violet loved being around people. When she was a child, her parents had allowed her to stay up late whenever guests were present, even at business functions for her father's work importing expensive textiles for high fashion suits and dresses. Sometimes they even asked her to play the piano as entertainment, which she never tired of.

Even at such a young age, Violet was always able to keep up with proper adult conversation, and friends would often remark at what a fun and clever young lady she was and what a lovely wife she would someday become.

Her debutante ball couldn't be coming at a better time, either, as Violet's childhood home had recently and irrevocably changed for the worse.

Daddy died just over a year ago when a devastating case of cholera swept through the city, taking thousands of lives all at once; Violet had even heard a distressed man remark that if the epidemic were to continue much longer, there wouldn't be enough men left alive to bury the dead.

It was horrible. The image of his yellow skin and the sound of that rattling cough still haunted her nightmares. No matter how hard Mama had tried to keep her from seeing such a ghastly sight, one glimpse of him was enough to burn into her memory forever.

Within days, the doctor had come to tell her and Mama that he hadn't made it through the night, that his body, clothes, and bed sheets needed to be removed from the home and discarded immediately, and that it was best they were not there to see it.

Mama took her to the water to watch the riverboats come in, and when they returned to their beautiful home on Rue Dauphine mere hours later, the house seemed entirely different. The lavishly furnished parlor looked the same. The grand piano still sat in the corner, its ivory keys reflecting the ray of sun that streamed inside. The shutters on the tall windows, which Daddy had painted a bold shade of violet in celebration on the day she was born, still stood there, sturdy as ever. But somehow, scrubbing the house of all of his things had made the home feel smaller. It was as if it had always been a home for two, and Daddy had never lived there in the first place.

Mama wasted little time in marrying again. Violet felt resentment and pity toward her mother at the same time. Surely the women of New Orleans would observe the fact that Mama had chosen to forgo the traditional one-year mourning period and judge the entire family for it.

On the other hand, Mama had responsibilities, and Violet was enough of a grown-up to know it. Some widows would waft through life as dark silhouettes in their black lace veils, fainting with grief at the briefest mention of their deceased loved ones while their brothers took care of the money and servants took care of the children.

But Mama had a business to run. She had no brothers, no adult sons, and little in savings. They had done well in New Orleans, but their status was as precarious as the town's interest in luxury fabrics; it never failed, but it did waiver, especially in times of war and disease, which had dominated most of Mama's life. If she wanted to keep the family afloat, well dressed, and part of civilized society, she was going to need a man to help.

General Boudreaux had led troops to victory in the Battle of New Orleans twenty years ago, which made him a celebrity of sorts. He was well respected for his devotion to the city, widowed by the same cholera outbreak that had claimed Daddy's life, and nearly alone now that his children had grown, married, and moved away, save for one: Justine, only slightly younger than Violet, who became her new and quite unwelcome step-sister.

Oh, Justine just drove her mad! She was a spoiled little socialite whose manners only appeared when the General was present, and the second he would turn his back, that devilish little smile would appear, the one that said "I can get whatever I want." She borrowed Violet's dress without asking and acted hurt when Violet told on her, claiming she just wanted them to be the kind of sisters who shared with one another. Then she cried and cried until Mama gave Violet a stern lecture and the General sent her to bed without supper. Once, Justine even took credit for doing chores the housekeeper, Della, had really done and earned herself an extra slice of cake for dessert.

The General may have led his men to victory on the battlefield, but he was a damn fool in his own home. Violet understood why Mama needed him, but that sure didn't mean she had to like him or his wretch of a daughter.

She wouldn't be marrying a gullible buffoon like him. Her future husband would be warm and generous, but also a quick-witted, respectable man who could run his home and his business with wisdom and sensibility.

That was the one thing she and the General could both agree on: it was time for her to find a husband. There was no shortage of eligible bachelors in a city as big as New Orleans, and if she had anything to say about it, she'd have suitors lining up at the door in no time at all.

Violet peered out her window at the beautiful, bustling city below. This Carnival would be the best one yet. In two short days, her life would officially begin.

* * *

She leapt out of her bed just as the sun graced the cobblestone streets beneath her window. One day to go before her ball, and there was much to be done.

Breakfast was simple: eggs, bread, grapefruit and tea. She sat across from Justine, with Mama at one end of the table and the General at the other.

"Darling," Mama said, breaking the uncomfortable silence the newly integrated family usually endured while they ate. "We have something to tell you." She shifted uneasily in her seat and straightened her posture. "It has been decided that Justine will be joining you at the ball tomorrow evening."

"As a –"

"Debutante, yes," the General answered, cutting her off. "We will be introducing both of you."

"But–"

The General shot an icy glare at Mama, who then sent the same glare to her. His chief complaint about Violet had always been her voice. In his eyes, she spoke too frequently when proper young ladies such as herself were supposed to listen and be agreeable to the authority figures in the room. As far as he saw it, it was Mama's failure to properly discipline her as a child that posed the greatest risk to finding her a suitable husband.

She desperately wanted to protest, but she knew there would be no arguing today. This was not fair. Justine was half a year her junior and would have her time soon enough! The next Carnival, even, would be appropriate for a girl her age. Daddy would never stand for this and she silently resented Mama for her acquiescence to this plan. The General may have been the man of the house, but it was *her* house to begin with.

Justine smirked over a spoonful of grapefruit, and Violet seethed.

After breakfast, Justine always went to the garden to study French, which was hardly fair; Violet wanted to be in the garden, it was the nicest part of the family's whole property. But no, Justine didn't want to be disturbed during her studies, and Violet would instead go read or practice piano in the parlor.

Not today. Justine was going to be disturbed whether she liked it or not.

"Why are you doing this to me?" Violet demanded as soon as the wooden screen door banged shut behind her.

Justine's eyes opened wide like baby deer. "I'm not entirely sure what you mean, sister," she said with a mock dramatic tilt to her head.

"Don't call me that!"

Justine shrugged. "What can I say? Father's a powerful man and people want to meet his youngest daughter. It's not always about you, Violet. I'm afraid that's just all there is to say about it."

Justine went back to her book and Violet wanted to tear those big eyes right out of her head. She could just picture Justine on the dance floor in a white gown like hers, smiling and greeting everyone and allowing them to overlook the other daughter of the house - the older daughter who had the right to be there while Justine very clearly did not.

A dress... Justine must already have a dress. It was far too close to the day of the ball to make her a new one now, and that meant Justine had known about this for some time.

Violet stomped back into the kitchen and retrieved a knife from a drawer, then thundered up the stairs to the room she had played in as a girl before she'd had to give away all her childhood possessions to make room for Justine.

There it was, hanging in the armoire. It was beautiful. Violet had chosen her own tasteful white gown months ago and had spent every day since dreaming of the moment she would get to wear it, but now it felt plain compared to Justine's much more expensive ensemble.

A pair of delicate lace gloves sat on a shelf beside the gown. Violet had heard Justine speak of those gloves before and knew they had belonged to Justine's mother. For a moment, she considered stealing the gloves instead, but that wouldn't be enough. Justine deserved to know how it felt to be stabbed in the back. And if Violet couldn't stab her step-sister, the dress would have to be the next best thing.

*   *   *

Violet felt satisfied for a minute or two after she heard Justine's conniption fit an hour later, but Mama, feeling just terrible for Justine, had gone to the shop on Rue Royale, fetched the most expensive fabrics they had, and spent the rest of the day making Justine's dress even prettier than it had been in the first place. Mama had even gone so far as to make a rose out of French lace to match Justine's mother's beautiful gloves, stitch it to the waist, and make her a special red ribbon to tie in a bow underneath it.

Mama was an intelligent woman; she knew what Violet had done and Violet would certainly catch a beating for this later, plus would have to say about a hundred or so Hail Marys in church next week, but she couldn't punish Violet by keeping her home from the ball. No story in the world would offer a sufficient explanation as to why the family would not present Violet, and Mama was in no mood to invite a scandal onto the family.

While Justine and Mama fixed the gown, Violet's mind furiously raced with worst-case scenarios for the upcoming ball. Justine was no fool; she'd know exactly what to do to make sure she charmed the most eligible young men like no one else in the room. Where would that leave her? Competing for the attention of the bachelors Justine didn't want, that's where. The boys with ugly hair and sweat stains under their arms, whose bellies were already stressing the buttons of their vests.

No, she decided, this could not be. God may have taken away her father along with hundreds of others who succumbed to that awful disease and there was nothing to be done about that. But God didn't want her to endure such a dreadful humiliation - the General did. And that was something she just couldn't accept.

She waited until after supper, when the sun had gone down and the servants began to light the lamps throughout the house.

Once the family had settled into the parlor for the evening to unwind from the usual troubles of the day, Violet politely announced that she was overtired from the excitement of the upcoming ball and would retire to bed extra early to read her scriptures and pray for her big day.

It was almost the truth.

Instead of heading up the stairs, she quietly slipped through the kitchen and out the back door, creeping across the potted palmettos in the garden and out through the wrought iron gate.

It was cold and dreary outside, but Violet hadn't had the time to retrieve her cloak. Visitors to New Orleans never expected the cold. They all thought of the South as being hot and sticky, but the city was known to succumb to the occasional cold snap in the winter months, and the wet, frigid air could whip across the river and wrap itself around a person, seeping under their clothes and straight into their blood. It did so this evening for Violet as she walked under the sycamore trees, past all the beautiful mansions on Rue Chartres, and into the bustling city nightlife.

One of the many details that made New Orleans the greatest city in the world was its fascination, bordering upon obsession, with many forms of spiritualism: the psychic fortune tellers, the Voodoo priestesses, the creyentes who practiced Santería - all of them thrived in the city she called home. Violet was a good church-going young lady, but her worldly, inquisitive mind led her to idolize the transfixing practitioners, most of them women, who claimed to communicate with what they cryptically referred to as The Other Side.

Some used cards or bones, some used fire, some even practiced elaborate rituals involving loud music and dance, and Violet admired the theatricality of it all. Violet's church had often denounced such practices, but nevertheless, modern-day spiritualism was all the rage, and New Orleans had certainly made itself known as the epicenter of the phenomenon.

Violet entered the Vieux Carré and passed by Congo Square, a site where slaves could gather and dance to the music of their homeland. When she was little, Daddy would bring her near here and treat her to a lemon ice while they watched the riverboats sail by on the Mississippi, and one time they passed a huge celebration in the square. It was loud, but gosh, it sure was beautiful.

As they walked past the iron fence surrounding the revelers in the park, she spotted a beautiful African woman, tall and slender with a yellow tignon in her hair. Her eyes were closed, her hands reached high in the air toward the sky, and wrapped around her shoulders was a long, heavy, green snake.

It looked right into Violet's eyes as she passed by. She had never seen a live one before, only heard of them in tales the grown-ups would tell of excursions into the swamps with deadly creatures lurking in the trees and on the banks of the bayou. Their eyes stayed locked for what felt like eternity, the creature's sinewy neck lifting its heavy head to stay right at Violet's eye level as she walked by, their gaze unbroken until Daddy hurried her along down the busy street.

The snake had scared her, that was certain, but the sight of it sparked something else in her, too. A force seemed to well up in her chest when she imagined those black eyes; something that made her insides feel stronger and her words sharper. It was a kind of confidence she never felt among her family at home, where she was bound every second of every day by the expectations of what a young lady were or were not to do.

She thought of this as she made her way to the alley behind the butcher's shop. There, she would find a lady who could make things happen.

* * *

For a few dollars, Celine could fix just about any problem Violet had.

The small room was dark, even though it had no door – just a thick red curtain separating the shop from the alley behind it. Violet sat across from her at a wooden table and tried not to stare at the collection of oddities around the room.

The walls were adorned with shelves holding various glass jars filled with claws and bones from small animals, rocks and crystals, oils and perfumes, gris-gris bags, and many, many candles. In the back corner behind Celine, a human skull sat on a tiny wooden table, surrounded by hand-rolled cigarettes and silver coins.

Violet wanted to know who she was, where she lived, and how

she had come to practice her craft, but there was no time for that. This visit was strictly business, and Violet's curiosity was of no use to the task at hand.

Celine clutched a cigarette in one hand and held out the palm of the other without a word. Violet dutifully paid her. Violet would have no need to earn her own money, but the women of New Orleans who performed this kind of service were able to make a living doing so, and that impressed Violet to no end. Women like Celine were simply better than most other people; cunning, otherworldly, and the kind of citizens who made New Orleans the spectacular place that it was.

"What brings you to my shop today?" Celine asked. She was a striking Caribbean woman with smooth skin and brown eyes that shimmered with just a hint of green.

"I need to make someone go away," Violet replied.

"How badly?"

"So badly. I want her far, far away from here."

"A young lady your age should scarcely have such powerful enemies."

"I only have one," she responded, "and once she leaves me be, I intend to have no others for as long as I live."

Celine took a long drag of her cigarette, the tiny embers brightening up her already sparkling eyes. The white smoke gently curved around her face and she met Violet's gaze as though she were going to ask another question, but remained silent.

Finally, she stood up to retrieve a small satchel from a nearby shelf and handed it to Violet, who curiously started to open it and inspect its contents, but was suddenly overcome by a need to get Celine's permission to do so first.

"Go ahead, look."

Violet gently poured a grainy black substance into her hand.

"Sand?"

"Black salt," Celine corrected. She took her seat again at the table and placed several more items in front of Violet: three large black candles, a book of matches, a small poppet made of burlap, and a folded slip of paper.

"Find the large cross at the cemetery crossroads and read it tonight when the streets are quiet," she instructed. "You will need something belonging to this person. Hair is good if you can find a comb they have recently used, but it would be best to include another personal item as well. It should be white, if possible, and something meaningful. Something they wouldn't want taken away from them."

Violet nodded and stood to leave.

"One more thing," said Celine. She retrieved a small skull from another shelf on the wall and set it down on the table, facing Violet. Violet shifted the other items to cradle them in one arm and picked it up. It was a familiar shape. It had belonged to a snake.

"Do not get carried away," Celine warned. "Follow the instructions as written. Tell the spirits what you want and be done with it. Should you find yourself in over your head, I shall not be there to protect you. Do you understand?"

Violet nodded. This may have been a new undertaking for her, but the confidence this plan inspired within her made her feel as tough as a knight in heavy armor. She knew all she needed to know to take charge.

*   *   *

It wasn't exactly silent in the graveyard, even if it was nearly midnight; New Orleans never was, and especially not on the eve of an event as highly anticipated as the Carnival. The beating heart of the city never stopped, and it was this very energy Violet loved so dearly about her home.

Violet had had no trouble finding hair in Justine's room. The oblivious little fool was sound asleep as Violet crept in to retrieve it; so soundly, in fact, that Violet took her time perusing Justine's bedroom in search of a personal item to borrow. Her eyes nearly turned red with rage when they landed on the fabric Mama had acquired for Justine's dress - fabric taken from the Davenport family business. Oh, yes, this would do nicely. This was something of hers that Justine had foolishly believed she deserved.

Now the red ribbon sat in front of her on the cemetery ground. Tucked between two heavy mausoleums, Violet found a patch of wet grass among the paved paths that cut through the St. Louis Cemetery as if it were its own little town.

New Orleans was positively deluged with the presence of the dead. The slippery mud and the water that raged just beneath the surface of the earth made it impossible to keep bodies underground, and therefore, they had to be interred above ground and remain alongside the living.

Violet shivered in the cold as she set up the three candles to form a circle around her and lit them with a match. She clawed at the damp ground with her bare hands to make a shallow hole in the earth and felt the dirt against her fingertips, cold and soft from the dreary, humid air, but not so damp as to have turned to mud. She sprinkled the black salt in a circle around it, then adorned the site with the snake skull as though it were a crown.

With a great deal of concentration, she wrapped Justine's stray hairs around the poppet as though she were wrapping a precious gift in silk, placed it in its shallow grave, and gathered herself to recite from Celine's handwritten note.

> *I call upon the spirit world*
> *To open its locked door*
> *I ask for Justine to leave this place*
> *And to speak to me no more*
> *No need for good-bye*
> *No need to fight*
> *No grudges from before*
> *I ask for her to leave this place*
> *And be banished evermore*
> *Earth and Heaven, fire and sea*
> *All eyes tomorrow will be on me*

She covered the poppet with the cool dirt and blew out the candles, one by one. Celine's instructions said to bury it on the outskirts of town, but as late as it was, Violet felt the need to return home and get as much rest as she could before the busy day arrived. This was far enough from home and would do just fine.

The instructions also said to leave the item with the poppet, but that wouldn't work for Violet - she needed to return it, lest Justine figure out it had gone missing and blame her for it. She *would* point the finger at Violet, too, just to make Violet's day even worse. The ribbon would be returned and Justine would be none the wiser.

Her bed felt as warm and soft as ever as she crawled into it. Outside, the streetlamps cast a soft glow over the city that patiently awaited her presence in the morning.

* * *

Her body tensed up and she woke with a jolt, her eyes shooting open in the dark. A stifled gasp stuck in her throat. Her whole body felt like a violin string pulled so tight it was just about to snap.

What was that? A noise? A voice? Something must have woken her, but it was still the dead of night, and the room was dark save for the glow of the streetlamps outside.

The floorboards made a gentle squeak as her bare feet touched them. She shivered and reached for her night coat, then slowly and nervously opened the door to her bedchamber, afraid of what might be on the other side.

Her logical mind tried desperately to tell her there was nothing to fear. She was about to be a married woman, and a fear of the dark was for little girls.

But her insides turned to ice when she opened the door and saw him standing there in the hallway: a tall figure, dressed in black robes with a blood red vest and a white ascot, his face obscured by a black mask with a long nose and a captain's hat covering his head.

He made no sound. Nothing shone from behind the mask, not even the slightest glimmer of reflection in his black eyes. He stood perfectly still, without so much as a gentle rise and fall of his chest or shoulders as he breathed - *if* he breathed.

Violet's breathing stopped as well.

For a moment she convinced herself she must be dreaming, but her heart pounded so violently inside her, she felt as though someone was repeatedly punching her in the chest. The pain and the tension in her entire body told her she was very much awake, and even if she could convince herself this man was an illusion, a trick being played by her tired eyes in this dark, narrow hallway, the fear that gripped her throat told her this was no apparition. He was a force of something dark, something inhuman, and he was here just for her.

* * *

Standing in front of him, she couldn't speak or even scream. All she could think to do was simply close the door and wait for the morning light to save her, banishing the darkness of night and with it the terrifying figure that had invaded her home.

She lay on her back for the rest of the night, staring straight into the ceilng, her eyes occasionally darting toward the door, which was now covered by a very heavy armoire that she had taken great pains to push in front of it at the expense of the once-pristine wood floor. Mama would surely give her Hell for it later, but for today, it didn't matter.

Slowly, minute by minute, the room became brighter as the dawn crept onto the windowsill. Before she knew it, there was a knock at the door.

"Miss Violet, breakfast is ready downstairs!" Della called to her.

She was surprised by the intrusion. Her plan had been to wait until the sun was up and the Louisiana heat began to fill the room, then check the hallway again. Another thought hadn't entered her mind in hours, not even of the rest of her family and whether anyone else in the house would encounter him.

Della attempted to open the door, but it banged against the armoire.

"Thank you Della, but I don't need help this morning. I'll be down shortly."

She quickly changed into a simple purple dress and tied a blue ribbon in her hair. Now the hard part: moving the armoire out of the way. She pushed as hard as she could, finding the task much more difficult now without the sensation of adrenaline rushing through her veins. Eventually it budged, little by little, leaving even more scratches on the floor beneath it.

Her pale hands trembled as she touched the cold brass doorknob and gently twisted it, opening the door with wide eyes and bated breath. Nothing graced the hallway but the faint voices coming from the dining room downstairs.

Whatever it was, it had gone away, just as she had hoped. Violet exhaled and gave control for the rest of the day to God. She had done her part, and perhaps this figure was just Celine's messenger, a way to tell her the forces were watching over her and everything was going to be just fine. Better than fine - the spirits wanted her to relish every moment of this day, and that was exactly what she intended to do.

The rest of the day went by in a blur. Hired ladies in simple attire buzzed around Violet for hours, hemming her gown, pinning her yellow hair in curls, painting her cheeks and eyelids, filing her fingernails, and pulling her corset as tight as they could manage.

Violet loved every moment of it.

But her mood soured every time she heard an obnoxious giggle coming from down the hall, where the very same treatment was being given to Justine.

Justine, with her raven hair and her sharp cheekbones being kissed with a maroon blush, her newly gussied-up white dress, and the red ribbon Mama had made special just for her.

She forced herself to smile bigger every time she heard the commotion coming from Justine's room. This would be her night, she reminded herself. She just had to be patient.

* * *

The hotel was one of the tallest buildings in town and had a second story ballroom large enough for nearly all of the city's upper class, and it was nearly filled to the brim with luscious white flowers that reflected the light of many exquisite candelabras.

Lining up with all the other debutantes atop the ballroom's grand staircase, perfectly poised in her white satin gown, upper length gloves, and Mama's prized pearls, made her feel like a perfect ballerina waiting for the curtain to lift so she could be admired by her adoring audience. Until, of course, so many of the city's most devoted fathers took their place beside their girls, ready to hear their family names announced by the emcee below and walk their daughters down the stairs and into the new world of adulthood.

Suddenly, it wasn't just resentment for the General she felt, but a longing so deep and painful it were as if she had been kicked in the belly by a mule. Daddy wasn't just absent from today's festivities. He was gone from every happy moment Violet would have for the rest of her life.

They would look ridiculous walking down the staircase with one of them on each of the General's arms. Only once had that happened before in Violet's lifetime, when the Moncrieff family had presented their twin girls some eight or nine years earlier, and that was entirely different; the whole city had scarcely ever seen the girls apart. They had worn their matching dresses at church every Sunday and shared every birthday cake, so naturally they would walk together with their father to make their debut. Justine was hardly Violet's other half - she was hardly even Violet's sister. She was an intruder.

Then, a sickening feeling came over Violet. The man on the stage downstairs was about to announce the daughters of the Boudreaux family - the General's family. Not the Davenports. Justine wasn't the intruder here. She was.

Sure enough, the Boudreaux family name was called and the three of them walked down the stairs, arm-in-arm.

It was...quick. As more family names filled the room, Violet found herself surprised by how simple it had been. Months of preparing for this moment, and it was over after mere seconds on a staircase.

No matter. The party was the fun part, anyway.

Once the hopeful young women in white gowns had taken their places around the dance floor, the champagne finally began to flow and music filled the room. Violet had expected a string quartet, but they had hired what must have been close to a full orchestra along with an honest-to-God opera singer. Until tonight, Violet had only imagined what an opera singer's most impressive vocal chords could sound like after Daddy and Mama returned from the opera house and Mama told her all about it as she put Violet back to bed. And her voice was just divine!

Champagne in hand, she took in the music and the sea of black suits and white gowns around her and darn near forgot all about the troubles that had plagued her mere moments before. Justine, who? She and the General and her annoying laugh could all go to Hell.

It was when the opera singer hit a high note and held it for at least the length of time it would have taken Violet to down a whole glass of champagne that she felt the color drain from her cheeks and her insides freeze. The hair stood up on the back of her neck. Her heart raced faster than the river after the summer rains.

She slowly looked over her shoulder and saw him standing there at the back of the room, taller and darker than any of the other guests. Those black eyes shone through his mask and stared straight at her, and it was then that she remembered seeing those eyes once before, when she was trapped in the gaze of the snake in Congo Square. Except now that feeling of confidence was gone, and only a paralyzing sense of dread remained.

Their eyes locked until a young couple passed her in the crowd, and a split second later, he was gone. She felt it in her blood that he was still here, and even if she couldn't see him, he could most certainly still see her.

The orchestra played on and the merriment continued, but to her, the room suddenly felt quiet. Something about it had changed. Then she realized what was missing: Justine's laugh. It had stopped.

Violet scoured the room looking for her and found nothing. She wanted to be glad that Justine had left the party, most likely taking a stroll with some potential suitor or another and finally leaving her to make her rightful choice in peace. But something held her back. She was afraid.

The General caught her eye. He was also searching the room, a look of consternation settling on his face. He leaned over ever so slightly to whisper something to Mama, who immediately afterward adopted the same expression and the same motion. They were looking for Justine, too.

"My, it sure seems as though our guest of honor is lost in her thoughts this evening," said a smooth voice. A smile involuntarily made its way onto her pink lips.

She turned to face Benjamin St. Claire, the eldest son of the owner of a lumber mill and member of the New Orleans city council. Benjamin would make a fine husband, indeed! He was, in fact, near the top of her list of eligible young men, and here he was, looking like a prince in his tuxedo, patiently standing there, awaiting her reply.

The rest of the room faded into obscurity.

"Perhaps," he continued, no doubt due to the length of time at which she stood frozen in place, staring at him, "you would not mind enlightening me as to what so thoroughly occupies your mind."

"Yes!" she blurted, and noticed he slightly bristled at the abrupt answer. "Um, certainly. Yes. Yes, that would be lovely."

"Splendid." He smiled and offered his arm.

* * *

The doormen opened the French doors to the terrace, and with them, the gates to another world.

The Carnival on the street below raged underneath her feet. Men dressed as court jesters did cartwheels and back flips or breathed fire on the street corners, the liquor flowed like water, and music poured from every open window in town. Mardi Gras celebrations had taken place when she was a child, but this was something else. Something raw, something spectacular.

Women danced with their midriffs showing. Dogs ran through the streets, barking. Every single man and woman wore a mask covering their eyes - sometimes even their entire face. It was as if everyone in New Orleans had been given permission to be someone - no, some*thing* - else, if only for this one magnificent night.

And here they all were, reveling and dancing beneath her as she stood above them on the wrought iron balcony as if she were their queen.

"Oh, my...I apologize, I had not realized the festivities had already become so..." Benjamin noticed a man and woman in the entrance of an alley down the street. They kissed passionately and the man pawed at the woman's breasts.

"...risqué. Perhaps inside would be better—"

"No!" Violet remarked, startling herself. "This is lovely, don't you agree? The air is so thick you can practically smell the magnolia trees from uptown. And the Carnival, well...I think it's just magical."

Benjamin stood up as straight as he could. "Very well. So, Miss Davenport, how do you find—"

She jumped as a shadow appeared across his face. Suddenly there was no light coming from inside the ballroom, and it was as if Benjamin, in his black suit and top hat, had folded into the darkness.

"Are you all right, Miss?"

She reached out to the direction of his voice and touched his face, confirming he was there even though she could no longer see him. He gently placed his hand on top of hers as the shadow disappeared, and there he was, her handsome suitor, gazing straight into her eyes. She knew she should remove her hand - what on earth would Mama say if she were to step out onto the gallery? - but the moment was just too precious.

Benjamin would propose, she knew it right then and there. They would live in a grand house with a large magnolia tree in the yard. They would come to the Carnival every year with their friends while their happy children slept soundly in their beds, protected by their loyal and adoring servants. Benjamin would take over the family business. He was young and educated with enough energy to bring the company forward and expand it as New Orleans continued to grow and prosper. The picture was as clear to her as anything she'd ever imagined.

So transfixed was she in the moment, she didn't notice the

droplet land on her wrist, nor the next one. But when the thick liquid began to trickle down her forearm, she couldn't ignore it any longer.

Benjamin looked at it, puzzled. "Miss Davenport, are you hurt?"

She examined her arm more closely. It was stained with blood.

And then, the scream.

She felt a surge of resentment toward whatever it was that broke the spell she had just shared with Benjamin. What stuffy socialite had ruined her evening with such a horrible sound? It was probably all for nothing - this woman, whoever she was, had no doubt seen a mouse. She had to get Benjamin's attention again. It had been nothing but pure luck that the two of them had had such a brief moment of privacy to begin with.

But just as Benjamin grabbed her hand and pulled her back inside to investigate the commotion, she looked up over her shoulder. A long ribbon dangled from the terrace on the floor above, and draped over the edge, lifeless and soaked in blood, was a hand covered in a delicate lace glove.

The musicians had stopped playing, but the room was louder than ever, filled with murmurs and gasps. A small group of men made their way down the crowded grand staircase. One of them carried a woman, her gloved arms wrapped around his neck, as she sobbed uncontrollably into his shoulder.

Violet felt the darkness creep upon her as she realized who the distressed woman was. It was Mama.

The ribbon hanging from the terrace was Justine's.

The realization crashed into her mind and made her feel physically ill. She hated Justine, but she didn't want her to die! And Justine was most certainly dead; a minor wound would not cause blood to spill in such a way that it could drip like that. Something terrible had happened and she knew in her heart that it had something to do with the snake.

Violet thought back to the night before and of the poppet buried in the cemetery. Celine had said to bury it away from town to make Justine go away, but Violet had disregarded that particular instruction and left her with the dead. Then, as if that hadn't been bad enough, she had brought the cursed object back to Justine instead of leaving it with the doll.

She felt light headed. She hadn't slept the night before and felt a wave of exhaustion rush over her. It mixed with her terror and made her feel as though she was trapped in a hideous nightmare. But a nightmare could never be so frightening.

She heard a sudden gasp next to her, immediately followed by a gurgling noise. Just beside her stood the opera singer, struggling for air as her gown became soaked in blood streaming from a stab wound to the neck. She collapsed on the floor and blood poured over the rug at Violet's feet.

Another scream from across the ballroom interrupted the one about to emerge from Violet's throat. Another debutante in her once-immaculate white gown collapsed, splattering blood across the wall as she fell.

Panic erupted in the room and several guests stumbled to the floor; whether they were trampled, fainted, or had succumbed to the same terrible fate as Justine, Violet did not know. The party descended into chaos all around her as everyone rushed to the door.

Standing there, perfectly still in the middle of the maelstrom was the dark figure with those cold, dead eyes. The world seemed to freeze around Violet. The room fell silent, and for a brief moment, no one else existed but the two of them.

Very slowly, he raised his hand as if to wave to her from across the room - only it wasn't a human hand at all, it was a blade of some kind, as black as the rest of him and dripping with blood.

Her trance was broken when the stampede of the crowd nearly lifted and carried her to the exit. Everyone was packed so tightly in the narrow stairwell they nearly suffocated against one another as they desperately tried to escape.

Violet tried to shove her way through the wall of bodies, but it was no use. She was being crushed by the mob and struggled to stay on her feet lest she fall and be trampled to death.

Finally, the flood burst through the bottom of the staircase and Violet ran through the hotel lobby and out the front door.

Expecting relief, she instead found the wind knocked out of her by being thrust from one crowd into another; the streets were packed with partygoers unaware of the tragedy that had unfolded beside them.

The screams from inside now blended with the music and excitement of the Carnival. It was a sea of silks and velvet, imitation pearls, glass gems, and bright colors; too bright, almost violently bright.

She looked around frantically and failed to find a familiar face. Staring at her instead was a menagerie of masks and disguises: beasts and birds, satyrs and mermaids - a cacophony of the natural and fantasy worlds in all their fascinating, beautiful, horrible, and even grotesque glory.

The masked strangers all seemed to be happy, laughing and shouting in French, German, Spanish, and every dialect of English, and many of them looked straight at her as they passed. Despite her torn and bloodstained dress, they laughed. Were they laughing *at* her? She suddenly felt smaller than she ever had, even as a child.

Then, she spotted him in an alley. Staring at her. Waiting for her.

Had she really done something wrong during the spell? Had she called upon the wrong spirit for help?

No, her intentions had been clear to her the whole time, and this was *not* what she wanted!

The fear that had gripped her entire body gave way to a white-hot rage. The source of her anger was something she could not quite decipher. She was furious at the General for making her feel inferior; at this demon, whatever he was, who misinterpreted her words and had wreaked havoc on this special occasion; at society itself for telling her that her value as a girl all came down to this night, a night that was now ruined, as was she.

She pushed her way onto the sidewalk, finally breaking free of the crowd. It turned away from her and ran - no, it *slithered* - down the alley.

Violet had never run so fast in her life. Her chest burned and her legs felt weak. But it was right in front of her, so close she could almost touch it - yes, her fingers grazed the cape that flowed in the wind behind him; she reached again and grabbed a handful of the soft fabric and pulled as hard as she could.

The figure came tumbling down onto the cold cobblestone street and she jumped on top of it, stomping her feet as hard as she could, then falling to the ground and pounding it with her fists.

"Leave this place!" Violet screamed at him, desperately trying to recall the words that had brought him here from the depths of Hell.

It raised its sharp appendage but did not have the chance to use it against her – Violet grabbed it, twisted it as hard as she could, and slammed it down into the creature's chest.

"I ask for you... no! I *demand* for you to leave this place and be banished evermore!"

Black sludge splattered over her face as she hit it over and over and over again, and the harder she hit, the more she felt the figure go limp beneath her hands.

It stopped moving. She stood and looked down at it, a pummeled mess in the middle of the cobblestone street. Her breath returned to her lungs and burned from the inside. The world around her that had turned a hideous shade of scarlet red came back into focus. And on the ground before her lay nothing but a black robe and mask.

The street behind her had gone completely silent.

As she slowly returned to the moment, Violet's gaze drifted over her shoulder. The whole town stood at the entrance to that dark, dank alley: partygoers, Carnival performers, noblemen, and debutantes alike watched her, aghast at the violent scene before them.

Just as she had commanded the night before, all eyes were certainly on her.

The General stood at the front of the mob, mouth agape, speechless and horrified. Violet's white gown and blonde curls were a mess of dirt, slime, and human blood. This was a hell of a sight to be seen, and it was how all of New Orleans would forever see her.

There was no explaining the ghastly sight before them and nothing for Violet to do but turn and face the city she loved, the city she knew she had betrayed with her own selfishness.

Consumed with shame, Violet could only think of retreating to her bed and allowing the sheer exhaustion of the ordeal to overtake her. What fate had in store for her tomorrow, she did not know, but she resigned to endure their judgments and accept whatever consequence found her the following day.

Violet stood still for a moment and stared back at them, then straightened her posture and smoothed her dress as best she could.

"Good evening," she said. "I'm rather tired. I think I'll retire for the evening now."

The crowd parted for her as she walked ahead.

The Acrobat

Somewhere in South Carolina

1841

Natalia danced.

When the cannons fired in the distance, Natalia danced.

When her baby brother cried from hunger, Natalia danced. When her mother left red marks on her backside, lashing out at her for God only knew what, Natalia danced.

Her little town of Siret suffered greatly under the rule of the Habsburgs. The people went hungry and the soldiers laughed at their pain.

Natalia was the child her family ignored. Her oldest sister, Marketa, was a grown-up in her eyes, shouldering the responsibility of caring for the younger ones while Mommy and Daddy took turns scrounging for food or drinking away what little money they had. Next were the twins, Stas and Vanya, boys who lived together in a community of two, as inseparable now as they had been in Mommy's womb. Then there was Natalia, then little Misha, the cub who still needed Mommy every second and who was too small for the grown-ups to look upon with frustration and resentment.

Natalia danced. Every time she heard music coming from another flat, or even when she didn't.

Eventually, Mommy and Daddy noticed her, realized that the town was just as hungry for any kind of entertainment as it was for food, and brought Natalia outside to dance in the streets. People tossed coins into Daddy's hat and sometimes the twins would sneak around in the crowd, scavenging for anything in unattended bags or pockets as onlookers watched the amateur ballerina twist and spin and stretch her body to the rhythm of songs the congregation would sing for her.

She did not mind it at first. Even outside in the snow, when the days were short and the crowds were small, it was still better than being cooped up in their empty flat, drowning in the sounds of grown-ups shouting and children crying.

But the older she got, the more unfair it felt that Mommy and Daddy would keep all the coins for themselves, sometimes buying whatever food they could for the family, but more often than not, disappearing for hours to find sad parties thrown in dingy basements to hide from the occupying forces.

Rumors swirled about neighbors who saved their pennies and fled to better places. Any place would be better than this and Natalia wanted to find one more than she had ever wanted anything. But she was going to need money to do it - money that she earned but never saw for herself.

Sometimes the injustice made her chest burn with anger, but she had learned the hard way to keep it buried inside her. One day, she lost control of herself and argued with Mommy. It was cold and windy and Natalia felt tired and sore from the dancing she had done the night before. She told Mommy "no" and Mommy yelled at her, then Natalia made the horrid mistake of yelling back. Mommy hit her on the side of the head with a tin pot, the only one they owned. Crusty bits of rice from the meager supper they had shared the night before stuck to her hair, and Mommy did not even let her clean up before shoving her out the door to dance again in the snow with blood trickling down the side of her face.

She danced in a shroud of humiliation and anger. It loomed over her, pressing down on her shoulders and throat. She held back tears. She hated them with all her being. But she danced.

She trailed behind her parents and siblings as they walked home that night and wondered how far she would make it in the woods with her small, tattered shoes and no food or water if she decided to make a run for it all alone.

The shadow grew heavy.

Then, she heard a voice.

"Good evening, *pasarea colibri*," he said to her. *Pasarea colibri* meant "little hummingbird," and the comparison filled her with joy. This stranger in the night saw her as a colorful, delicate creature that spent its life fluttering between beautiful things. He instantly had her attention.

"You are a lovely dancer," he continued. He spoke her native language, but with a heavy English accent.

Natalia, unaccustomed to being spoken to by anyone but her parents - and in any tone but a harsh one - did not respond, but simply nodded.

"Would you like to take a walk with me?"

She glanced at her building at the end of the block, the grey, concrete box with a faint candlelight shining from their corner flat.

"Just for a few minutes. A lap around the building, nothing more."

The lap around the building proved to be the most important

few moments of Natalia's life. By the time they arrived at her front door, Natalia had learned that the stranger's name was F.W. Scott and that he was a businessman in London who ran something called a circus, a cacophony of exotic animals and acts of wonder: dancers who could contort their bodies into unnatural shapes, acrobats who flew through the air on a web of ropes and wires, and even mystics who read minds to tell audiences what awaited them in their future. He was traveling through Europe to find talent and was lucky enough to find this little hummingbird here in the middle of nothing.

Best of all, the new circus Mr. Scott had in mind was not intended to stay in London but would tour all over America, and in addition to room and board, Natalia would be granted a small salary for her contributions, should she decide to accept his invitation.

To Natalia, it sounded like pure magic.

Without hesitation, Natalia met him at the edge of town the next morning and never looked back.

* * *

Mr. Scott had more scouting to do around Eastern Europe, so he sent her on a wagon with a guide - who hardly spoke two words to her the entire journey - to London to meet his American business partner, Harrison Monroe.

As the cart finally pulled up outside a grand hotel, he stood outside, waiting for her, as if he somehow knew the exact moment she had been due to arrive. He was a tall, blond man with bright blue eyes and wore a purple vest with a white ascot, quite the contrast to the sea of grey suits and bonnets worn by the other Londoners.

Their eyes locked as soon as Natalia stepped off the wagon, uneasy after so many grueling days and nights on such a hard, uncomfortable surface. She glided to him and looked up as he towered over her.

"You must be our new little hummingbird. Welcome, Natalia."

He studied her for a moment: her pale face, unwashed hair, tattered clothes, and frail body. He gently touched the scar on her temple where Mommy had hit her.

"What happened here?" He asked, cautiously.

She did not know how to answer in her own tongue let alone in her fractured grasp of the English language. The best response she could manage was a subtle shrug.

"I have a salve for that. It will help the scar fade. I imagine you must be hungry, though I'm afraid you are not dressed for any respectable restaurant. Come up to my room. We'll get you a proper bath and a meal, then I'll take you to find a dress or two before we leave tomorrow."

Mr. Monroe's room was luxury as Natalia had never imagined. There was a large white washbasin full of hot water and a collection of soaps that smelled better than any flowers that bloomed in Siret in the summer. Mr. Monroe gave her a silk robe to wear when she was done, and when she finally emerged from the washroom, her dinner had been prepared and set out for her on a table covered in white linen.

As she ate the generous helping of roast pork, green vegetables, and freshly baked bread, a wave of exhaustion overcame her, and she longed to rest in the bed across the room that was larger than the straw mattress she had shared with all four of her siblings. Mr. Monroe, seated across the table from her and sipping on a glass of expensive whiskey, seemed to read her mind.

"The ship leaves for America tomorrow evening," he explained. "That will give you plenty of time for a good night's rest and to find some proper clothes before we set sail with the others."

Natalia had assumed there would be others since Mr. Scott had been sending talent to Mr. Monroe from all over Europe. She wondered why they were not here in this hotel room with them, but her mouth was too full of food for her to bother asking.

"Of course, I'll need to see what you can do first. I'll need to see you dance. And see your body. And I'll need to be assured you can handle the physical exertion of the job."

Even though she understood perhaps half of the English words he spoke to her, she knew exactly what he meant.

She had not done it before, but was not so sheltered that she did not understand what it was or how men in his position used their authority to obtain it; the occupying soldiers in Siret had done as much to most girls in the village and Natalia figured that her exit had come at just the right time to avoid being subjected to such behavior herself. At least in this situation, she was gaining something from it.

Mr. Monroe gave her a sip of his whiskey to steady her nerves, then she disrobed for him and did all that he asked.

He held up his end of the bargain afterwards. The next day,

freshly bathed, rested, and wearing a new dress, she and a handful of others, whose talents were not yet obvious enough for her to know, set sail for America.

* * *

Time passed very quickly in the years that followed. Natalia and the rest of the circus renegades lived in decorated wagons pulled by horses, jaunting from tiny town to tiny town, never quite knowing where they were or what day it was. Some days there would be wind and snow; other days, scorching sun and heat. Some days she opened the wagon door to see the tent go up against a backdrop of majestic mountains, and on other days, the nothingness behind it seemed to stretch to the end of the earth.

Americans were particularly preoccupied with exotic animals, and this circus had a menagerie not to be seen in most other places in the country. But Mr. Monroe's vision was to expand far beyond simple viewing, as one could do in a museum, and entertain the masses with talents and oddities.

At present, the circus also featured Madam Lucille, the fortuneteller; Siamese twins, Otto and Orson; a man covered in tattoos that had since turned green all over his body (Mr. Monroe would oscillate between exhibiting him as The Tattooed Man or as "Irving the Lizard King"); Davey and Mikos, who juggled with dangerous objects like fire or knives; and Belinda the Snake Charmer, who had joined her on the ship to America some time ago and who had, unbeknownst to Natalia, brought four pit vipers with her in her suitcase that had thankfully never escaped.

At the center of it all was Natalia: the last act of every evening, the star of the show.

Natalia had been traveling across America for years, and in that time she had mastered every act that Harry - she called him Harry now - had asked of her and created many more.

She walked on tightropes, performed pirouettes on the backs of elephants, spun in circles in giant hoops that dangled from the rafters, and lifted her fellow circus workers high into the air as if she were lifting a doll. She did it all wearing a tight corset and pointed canvas shoes, covered in bright make up with ribbons in her hair, and she loved it.

Her favorite act of all was the trapeze. Swinging from one bar to the next, she defied the laws of Heaven and Earth, and the thrill of it meant nothing else in world existed in those precious moments. She was an angel. A goddess. A hummingbird.

The act had expanded from two horizontal bars to seven, with a wooden platform on either side and a rope ladder to climb up and down. It was simple, but it was all Natalia needed. She would swing and leap from one bar to the next, weightless and unafraid of the prospect of falling to the ground below.

It was only when she set foot back on the solid ground, when the audience would burst into applause and throw flowers at her feet, that Natalia would remember the presence of other people inside the giant canvas tent.

The recognition was a welcome change for Natalia. She kept the flowers and hung them in her dressing room long after they died. Her vanity was covered in red, pink, and yellow rose petals and beautiful shades of eye shadow and rouge. If not in the air or practicing alone outside, Natalia could be found here among her collection of brightly colored costumes and her very large mirror.

Oh, how she loved that mirror. Mommy never kept one in the cold, empty flat back in Siret, and until she joined the circus, she had been entirely unfamiliar with the sight of her own face. Even now, years after she had left that hopeless little town, she could not get enough of it. She spent some of her meager earnings from the circus on more exotic make up and changed the way her face looked, painting diamond shapes around her eyes or hearts on her cheek bones.

Before she had this mirror, she did not even know the color of her own eyes. Now she leaned over candles at all hours of the night staring into the galaxy of brown and grey and even little bits of green here and there.

The scar on her temple had faded, leaving only a faint white line where the damage had been. The woman Natalia saw in the mirror was not the girl who had danced in the snow in Siret.

Harry came by to visit from time to time. For the first few years, she longed for him when she slept alone at night, especially in the winter months, and resented every new girl who received the same treatment from Harry as she had in the London hotel room. Once the news of the circus had spread through certain parts of the country, Harry no longer found the need to travel to Europe in search of performers; rather, Americans with a talent to showcase came to him, and Harry had his pick of any young woman he wanted on a given night.

Nowadays, he came to her bed when he was experiencing a spell of boredom or loneliness, and otherwise, he only came to her dressing room to pay her at the end of the week.

Circus performers came and went from one season to the next. Some were rebellious runaways who joined to upset their parents, then went right back home when their point had been sufficiently proven. Some tired of the lifestyle and picked a dusty town in which to meet a handsome farm boy and settle down. Others moved on to new jobs. Many never offered an explanation at all.

Natalia did not bother getting attached to any of them. She did not see the point. Save for her own reflection, she mostly kept to herself.

A relatively new woman named Ida was someone she considered a friend, however - someone she even admired. Who wouldn't admire her? She was a lion tamer with the grace of a princess, the courage of a warrior, and the showmanship required to handle a wild beast and a hungry audience at the same time. She was one of the few young women who had not been made a temporary companion to Harry upon her arrival; so impressive was her skill with the lion, Harry needed no further convincing.

Even without the lion at her side, Ida was striking. Her wavy blonde hair was cut short and fell just below her ears, and due to the nature of her work, she always wore pants and equestrian boots like a lady - or like a gentleman, for that matter.

It was Ida who brought her the upsetting news that day.

* * *

The circus had been traveling around a land called South Carolina, and though Natalia was not in the habit of keeping track of where she had visited or how many times she had been there, she knew she hadn't toured through this place before. Something about this locale struck her as unusual.

It was warm here near the forests and the swamps. The humid air would hug her tighter and tighter, as if this were a place that wanted to wrap itself around her and never let her go. The trees seemed to open up and make room for the canvas tent, embracing it with their low hanging branches. The moss that draped from them swayed gently in the wind, and Natalia was overcome with the feeling that there were secrets in the trees, secrets they wanted her to know.

Something about those trees made Natalia think of the woods behind her village, the ones she had stared into every day and every night on her way to and from her corner on the street, longing to run to them, no matter what danger may have lurked behind them.

This land looked nothing like the dreary, brittle woods in Siret, but there was a weight to it that Natalia knew all too well. It was a world that held a restless agony underneath its stillness, a place as burdened by its own antiquity as she was.

Natalia awoke late that morning, slightly sore from her trapeze act the night before. They were done with whatever town this was and preparing to head onto the next. Large, grey clouds hung low in the sky and threatened to rain, which sent the workers scrambling to pack everything and get a move on.

It seemed to be taking an extra long time for them today, but Natalia did not care. She sat at her vanity, wrapped in one of her silk robes, and stared into her reflection, gently basking in the soft light of such a dreary day. She wished she could bottle the intoxicating scent of the mossy trees and rain and keep it on her vanity with her many other perfumes in their delicate glass bottles.

She carefully brushed her long, curly hair, the ringlets as tight as ever thanks to the heavy moisture in the air, then lathered her hands with lotion and took in the smell of the rain and the rose petals around her, when Ida entered, holding a tin cup of hot coffee.

Natalia and her reflection both turned to look at her.

"Good morning, doll," Ida said.

Natalia liked it when Ida called her that. It was not as good a nickname as "hummingbird," but it still made her feel delicate and special.

Ida handed her the coffee and she drank.

"I suppose you've heard the news."

News? Natalia shook her head.

Ida pulled a cigarette from the pocket of her jacket and lit it with a match.

"Half our workers left last night. I expect more will follow suit today." She took a long drag and exhaled a heavy sigh of resignation.

"Monroe won't be paying us anymore. Not for awhile, at least."

Without warning, Natalia was transported right back to the streets of Siret, dancing for a drunk and unruly crowd while her parents pocketed everything she had earned.

America had not had an easy time of it lately, she knew. The papers called it the "Panic of 1837," and while she did not understand what their banks had done or why the situation unfolded the way it had, she knew it resulted in a smaller number of onlookers at her shows. But that had been a few years ago now and the attendance was creeping back up to normal. More importantly, audiences were no less impressed by Natalia's achievements. She was doing her part, and if Harry was not going to pay her for it, he was weaseling out of their deal - it was as simple as that.

Natalia slammed her tin cup on the vanity, splashing coffee onto some of her treasures.

"I know, doll. I'm mad at the son of a bitch myself."

"Why? Why would he do this?"

Ida took another drag and shrugged. "All I heard was something about more circuses cropping up around the country and touring even farther than ours. One supposedly goes all the way from Montreal to Havana. So he won't be paying us until we step up our acts and compete."

Thunder suddenly rumbled across the countryside and rain began to wash over the wagon. Natalia hardly noticed. She had never heard of places called Montreal or Havana and she did not care where they were or how many circuses went there. She had a job to do and she had been doing it. The business end of the circus was Harry's problem, not hers.

But what choice did she - or any of them - have? The sideshow acts in particular had nowhere to go, so they would be staying put no matter what. In truth, the promise of a roof and a hot meal was plenty to keep most of them around.

Now, years after she had felt it on that cold night after Mommy hit her, here it was again, that heavy feeling of the shadow pressing down on her shoulders and tightening around her throat.

But no one was going to come out from the darkness to save her this time.

* * *

"Take a raincoat, at least!" It was the last thing Natalia heard Ida shout to her over the pouring rain as she stomped away from her wagon. Puddles formed as quickly as her bare feet made holes in the mud, soaking her legs and the bottom of her robe. The air was thicker than molasses and the mossy trees behind their camp seemed to sink under the weight of it.

The remaining workers did their best to load up the last of the wagons and hitch up the horses, preparing to point them to the nearest dirt road and onto their next adventure, supposing, of course, the wagon wheels would budge in this muck.

She walked straight past the enormous elephant cage, the gorillas, the bear, and Ida's lion, which she affectionately referred to as Oscar; past the fortuneteller, the illusionist, and the fire jugglers, until she reached Harry's office and stormed inside without bothering to knock.

"Tali, my goodness. You're soaked to the bone."

She glared at him.

Even though each wagon was exactly the same in size and texture, Harry's office – which also happened to be his bedroom, though there had never been much of difference between the two – somehow seemed darker than hers. His desk and furniture were all stained brown or black. Even the silver-framed mirror on the wall seemed to have a darker hue. But Harry liked to keep fresh flowers in the office, and the pink roses on a small table near the door were a welcome touch.

Harry checked his pocket watch.

"We're leaving any moment now. You had better get back to your wagon, lest you be stranded outside."

"No." She said, trying to keep her voice steady. "I will stay here until you pay me for the week."

He gave her a sly smile. "I suppose you've heard the news of our financial troubles."

"I do not care for your financial troubles," she said as a matter of fact. "People come, people pay, people watch, you pay me."

She held out the palm of her hand. He looked at her with pity.

"Oh, Tali, darling. Look at you. Dripping wet, freezing to the bone, your hair covering your pretty face, your palm outstretched, asking for pennies. I imagine you looked this way for so much of your life back in Siret. You poor thing."

"I do not need sympathy. I need money."

"What for? Hmm? Why do you need money? Do you think you will settle down someday and buy a little plot of land? Build a little cabin? Become a dairy farmer or something of the sort?" He laughed. "Darling, you have everything you need here and you know that. We are a family, and sometimes we need to make sacrifices for the good of our family, don't we?"

The family Natalia had had before was bad enough and she did not find herself in need of another one now.

Harry gently stepped away from her and poured himself a glass of whiskey from a crystal decanter on the desk.

"Tali, when I was a young man, my father worked as a printer for a small newspaper, and as soon as I was old enough to handle the machinery, he brought me to work with him. The town we lived in was quite small. So small, in fact, that when a case of influenza broke out among us, the population drastically decreased in a matter of weeks. My father was one of those lost to the epidemic, and I found myself, as a boy of thirteen, working twice as hard for a newspaper that was now on the brink of financial ruin. I was one of the few printers left. I worked until midnight, slept in a broom closet, and rose at dawn to do it all again, and I never complained. We make sacrifices for our work in America, Tali. We do what we must for the good of the company, and we become stronger for having done it."

Her throat tightened. What was the word in English? She couldn't find the word for a human snake.

"You must be cold. We'll be leaving soon, but since you're here, why not stay until our next stop? You can keep warm here with me." He pulled at the sleeve of her soaking wet robe and touched her bare shoulder.

Behind him, Natalia could see her reflection in the mirror on the wall. Her own eyes were staring into the back of his head and before she knew it, her reflection reached out for Harry's neck.

She had not even felt her own arms move, but suddenly, she had her hands tightening around his throat.

"Whoa there, *colibri*, take it easy! Such a strong grip from a delicate hummingbird."

Natalia immediately relented, unsure of what had come over her.

"You like it soft and slow, remember?" He leaned in to kiss her and she shoved him away, storming out of the wagon and slamming the door behind her.

The second she stepped into the mud, she slipped and fell. The rain was still coming down hard, and the thick, fragrant air suddenly felt oppressive.

As she tried to stand and find her balance, she heard the crack of a whip.

"No, no, no!" She cried to no one in particular. The horses began to clip-clop their way through the mud toward those huge, mossy trees that seemed to form a tunnel on the road ahead.

She ran to her wagon and scrambled to open the door. Her hand slipped off the knob and she nearly fell into the mud again, but she regained her composure and sprinted faster, leapt for the door once more, and managed to yank it open and dive inside as the caravan rolled away.

*   *   *

Natalia's own brown eyes stared back at her that night.

A small part of her wanted to refuse to perform until Harry paid her what was owed and promised never to betray her again. But that side of her was silenced by simple logic: Harry would do what he wanted and Natalia had no recourse to convince him otherwise.

Fixated on the sight of her own reflection, her mind darted back and forth between empathy for Harry's situation and a hot, seething rage.

If it were not for Harry, I would have starved back in Siret.

I am the star of the show. The circus is nothing without me.

It is expensive to feed and care for all of us.

We do this for a living. Not just for food. Harry knows this.

It is not his fault that times are hard.

Nor is it mine.

A soft knock at the door interrupted her argument with herself. Natalia turned her head toward the sound, unaware that her reflection did not follow suit.

"Come in."

"Strong crowd tonight," Ida said, and Natalia's heart welled with anger. A strong crowd meant a lucrative show, and a lucrative show meant Harry was a liar.

"You're up next. And you look beautiful," Ida told her.

Natalia knew this to be the truth.

"I guess your talk with Monroe didn't go so well?" Ida asked, and Natalia's silence was all the answer she needed. "Don't let him get you down," Ida said. "Just do your act for the audience, not for him."

"Why aren't you angry?" Natalia asked, almost as an accusation.

"I am," Ida replied. "I'm just not surprised. Why do you think I spend all my time with lions? They're a hell of a lot easier than men."

Natalia looked back in the mirror once more and was suddenly confused when she glimpsed the scar on her temple. It was much more obvious than she had noticed in a very long time.

"Ida, look here," she instructed. "Do you see a scar?"

Ida looked closely. "Not much of one. A tiny line, I suppose, but I never would have noticed it myself."

Applause began to roar from the tent outside. The previous act was done, and Natalia was up.

* * *

Natalia took her place at the top of her ladder just as the fire jugglers took their final bow. She gently closed her eyes and allowed the cheering crowd to melt away into nothingness. All Natalia could hear in that moment was the sound of her own breath.

Her hands stretched out ahead of her in anticipation for their contact with the first bar on the trapeze, and on the very first note played by the violins below, she fell from the platform, trusting them to lead her into her aerial ballet.

Back and forth she swung. She dangled in the air in her ballerina pose, pointing her toes and doing pirouettes on an invisible stage. She twirled and stretched and did somersaults as if the earth below her did not even exist.

She wrapped both legs around the bar and hung upside down, her arms reaching out to the side, and arched her back enough to grab her feet, forming her body into a circle. She swung faster and brought herself so high her hair nearly grazed the top of the canvas tent.

It was daring and dangerous to swing so high and with such momentum, but she held her form until, in one rapid motion, she let go and flipped her body to have her feet come below her, preparing to land back on the wooden pedestal in a pose that most resembled a hummingbird descending onto a flower.

But suddenly, against Ida's advice and her own intentions, she thought of Harry.

"My *pasarea colibri*," he said to her in her mind.

Her eyes shot open and for the briefest second, she thought she saw another acrobat on the platform across from her, posing in the same pirouette as Natalia.

She gasped. Her steady breathing was interrupted and she lost her balance, crashing against the edge of the platform, then tumbled down to the ground and landed hard against the dirt.

* * *

Natalia had managed to position her body to land as softly as possible, resulting, fortunately, in a bad sprain and nothing more. A part of her felt disappointed by the inevitable boredom she would face by being cooped up in her room and away from the tent, but a much more powerful side of her felt incredibly smug. Harry wouldn't have his star for a week or two, and that served him right.

A tiny scratching noise came from the other side of the wagon door, so soft Natalia paid it no mind until it was followed by a yowling sound.

Curious, she pushed herself up off the bed and hopped on her stronger foot to open the door. A small black cat came darting inside. It sniffed around the floor for a moment, and upon finding an acceptable spot, sat down and looked directly at Natalia.

"What do you want?" she asked the feline. "I have no food for you. Shoo!" She gestured toward the open door, but the cat lay down on its side, making itself more comfortable.

Out of the corner of her eye, she saw her reflection in the vanity mirror, its gaze also landing on the cat in the middle of the floor. But for a quick moment, Natalia's reflection appeared to smile at it.

A cold breeze drifted inside. The circus camp had settled near a river this time, and the wind carried a chill from the still water up to Natalia's wagon. She looked past the encampment to see the full moon shining brightly in the water, its reflection dotted with tiny lily pads and criss-crossed by the shadows of low hanging tree branches.

Another storm appeared to be forming over the countryside, and as the wind picked up and soared through those heavy trees,

Natalia could swear she heard whispering in the woods. Not words, not exactly, but soft, mournful cries.

She shivered. Natalia was not so heartless as to cast the poor little animal out in the wind and the rain, and there was no point in standing here with an open door, having a staring contest with a cat.

She shut the door and hobbled back to her position on the bed with her foot propped up on a pillow. The cat jumped up and cuddled beside her, gently purring as it nuzzled itself under her arm. She scratched its chin and quickly came around to the idea of the cat staying with her for more than just a stormy night.

* * *

When Natalia awoke the next morning, the cat was sitting on her vanity, staring into the mirror. She thought for a brief moment of bringing back a bowl of milk for it when she retrieved her own breakfast, but the thought was quickly extinguished by a surge of pain from her foot. It was far more swollen than it had been the night before, and without a crutch or a cane, there was no way she would be able to walk in search of a meal.

Natalia was not stupid. She had seen enough old ladies back in Siret to know that bodies did not stay young and beautiful forever. They wore out after years of hard labor, hunger, child bearing, and drinking. Some of the old ladies could not even walk to church anymore and relied on their children to care for them as if they were helpless little babies. Natalia had no children of her own and no intentions to breed, which meant that when her own body aged and refused to perform in the manner she had for so many years, she would be alone in the world.

And this was why Natalia needed money.

She would not turn into one of those old ladies, nor into a mean, miserable thief like Mommy or Daddy. She had built her livelihood on her talent and would not let it slip away from her. Not yet. Not while she was still young enough to make her own money fair and square.

She sat up and winced as she moved her foot to the floor. She would not be able to make it to the breakfast tent, but at the very least, she needed to find water. As she carefully lifted herself to stand, her reflection came into view. Spooked, the cat suddenly hissed - not at her, but at the mirror.

Natalia hopped over to the vanity chair on her good foot and the cat became even more agitated, arching his back and letting out a low growl.

"Oh, hush," Natalia snapped at him as she took her seat.

The cat looked at her, then at the mirror, then jumped off the vanity and ran underneath Natalia's bed.

Her door opened slowly.

"Knock, knock," said Ida. "Thought you might need this."

Ida held up a bowl of porridge and a tin mug of coffee. Natalia's heart swelled. Ida had thought to help without Natalia even asking, and it dawned on her now that no one had ever done such a thing before - not without expecting something in return, like Harry had. A hint of suspicion suddenly flashed through her mind, as if she were waiting for Ida to ruin the moment with a demand of some kind.

"You all right there, doll?"

Natalia snapped out of it and reached for the food. "Yes. Fine. I am hungry."

It was a cold, lumpy pile of mush that bordered on inedible, but Natalia ate it anyway.

"Let's take a look at what we have here, shall we?" Ida gently lifted up Natalia's swollen foot and set it on the vanity in front of her. "Oh, darling! That looks just awful! Does it feel as bad as it looks?"

"Yes," Natalia said with her mouth full.

"Oh, dear. If this is broken, you will need at least a month off to heal, perhaps two."

Natalia's eyes widened. Two months! Oh no, that would not be acceptable. Staying off the trapeze for a week or two would give her a respite from Harry's betrayal and disrupt his show, but a longer postponement would render her entirely useless to the circus.

"No!" Natalia cried. "Harry will not wait that long! He will replace me!"

Ida grew quiet.

"What is it?"

"I didn't think much of it this morning when I went to fetch breakfast, but..."

Natalia glared at her. "But what?"

"There's a line of girls outside Monroe's office. He usually attracts a lot of auditions these days, but these girls, well... they kind of look like you, with dance shoes and ballerina outfits... it seems as though he's looking to replace you already."

He had dancers here in the early morning, which meant he must have placed an ad in the local paper a day or two before. He intended to oust her not because she had injured her foot, but because she had confronted him on his betrayal.

She stood up and struggled to set her broken foot on the floor without placing weight on it.

"Honey, be careful!" Ida exclaimed.

Natalia reached for Ida's arm. "Help me," she said to Ida - the first time she had said that to any human being.

Ida was puzzled, but obliged.

She made it across the large, open field to Harry's trailer one step at a time, hobbling along with Ida's support. She pushed her way past the line of dancers and flung the door open, interrupting an audition with a teenage girl, no older than Natalia had been when she first met Mr. Scott.

She looked at the girl with disdain and one word managed to come from her mouth: "Out."

The girl shot a look at Harry, who motioned for her to stay put.

"Get out!" Natalia barked again.

"Tali, just the person I was hoping to see. I'd like you to meet Dorothy, our new acrobat."

Dorothy lit up with excitement; clearly, she had not been made aware of her success until this moment.

"Ida, be a dear and tell the other girls they can go home. And Tali, why don't you head back to your room and rest? I'll be by to further discuss this matter with you later on."

He turned his attention to Dorothy and placed both hands on her shoulders. "And you, my darling, congratulations. Please return here tomorrow morning at ten o'clock sharp. We will need to discuss your acts, get you on the trapeze, and of course, make sure you're up for the physical exertion of the job."

Dorothy beamed. Natalia erupted with rage.

The vase full of pink roses sat within Natalia's reach near the door. Without thinking, she grabbed it and hurled it straight at Harry's head. He ducked, barely, and the vase smashed against the wall, scattering pink rose petals and shards of glass all over the room.

Natalia stormed out as best she could with her imperfect

balance. Ida spit on the floor. "Pig!" she snapped at Harry, then slammed the door behind her.

Natalia did her best to rush back to her own wagon, tugging on Ida to hurry up and pull her faster.

"Slow down! You're going to hurt yourself again!" Ida pleaded, but Natalia did not care.

As soon as they made it to her door, Natalia pulled away. "Just leave me be," she said to her only friend as she stomped inside the wagon.

Natalia trembled with fury, her breath heaving, her teeth clenched together so tight she could have broken them. She wanted more than anything to scream, but the image of the metal pot hurling toward her face as Mommy hit her flooded her mind and forced her to keep the screaming inside. All she could do was cry.

She flung herself down on the bed and sobbed into her pillow. The cat, sensing her despair, hopped up onto the bed and curled up next to her. She gently pet him on the head, grateful for his concern.

With her face buried in the soft bedding, Natalia did not notice her reflection sitting upright, staring at her.

*   *   *

Hours passed. The gates opened, the crowds gathered, and the shows began. Natalia had cried herself dry and now clung to the simple satisfaction of knowing Harry would be without a headlining act for a while until Dorothy was properly trained. It had taken Natalia months to master each one of her acts and she was more talented than most. It would take this novice much longer to figure out what she was doing.

But it was of little consolation. She would need to find another place to live, another job, another life. This wagon would belong to Dorothy soon, though Natalia would be damned if she let her keep anything inside of it. Her bed, her costumes, her silk robes, her flowers, and especially the vanity and mirror were coming with her no matter where she went. Never again would she live in an empty room with ugly grey walls like she had in Siret.

She could stay near here for now. The landscape was scenic, the flowers filled the air with their sweet smell in the afternoon heat, and the homes they passed on their way through the countryside were beautiful mansions surrounded by large swaths of land; nothing like the cold, concrete buildings she had known as a child.

Natalia did not delude herself into thinking one of those lovely homes could be hers, but even a small flat in some little town nearby would surely be enough for her and her precious things. A girl like Natalia could get along just fine here without any help, and if she did not find this place to her liking after all, she could move on and start over as many times as she wanted.

But as she considered such a life, her heart filled with resentment. Why should she have to go *anywhere*? This was her home - a home she had earned many times over. She seethed with anger, but also felt helpless and desperate for Harry to see what he saw in her in London all those years ago. If she could just get his attention for one more show, Harry would understand that she belonged on the trapeze, broken foot or no broken foot.

Tonight, Natalia decided, she would prove it.

* * *

Davey and Mikos, the fire jugglers, were intended to be the last act of the evening in the absence of an aerial entertainer. The band was about to pack up for the night when they heard a whistle coming from the sky, and taking their cue like good musicians should, they played her song.

For the first time, perhaps ever, Natalia felt nervous.

She took an extra second to steady her breath, falling a beat or two behind the music. As she finally let go and glided into the air, she looked for Harry. Natalia had never concerned herself with the audience before - had never even noticed them until the very end of her act. The sudden awareness of hundreds of eyes watching her made her insides feel hollow. So far, Harry was nowhere to be found, and she worried that she was up here pushing through the pain of a broken bone for nothing. But even if he were not here, someone would tell him about this extraordinary effort. Wouldn't they?

The incessant thoughts were distracting her and she fumbled on one of the bars, nearly falling all the way to the ground below. A few in the audience gasped. She needed to focus. She swung her legs over the bar and hung upside down in her favorite pose, but the pain of placing weight on her damaged leg was agonizing.

She pulled herself up to a seated position and gently swung back and forth like a child on a playground. Just a few seconds - that was all she needed to find her center again.

But she nearly fell backwards when she noticed it.

Directly across from her on the far side of the truss and in the exact same position was the mirror image of herself. Another woman in her costume, with her hair and make up set in the same fashion, staring at her. *Glaring* at her.

This other woman had a sharp edge to her somehow, a kind of anger radiating from her body, but also possessed an unsettling, sly smile on her face.

Natalia used her weight to twist the ropes above her, then allowed them to unfurl and spin her in circles. The other woman did the same.

Natalia jumped from her seat and dove through the air, catching the next bar in front of her. The other woman did the same.

Was it Dorothy? It had to be Dorothy! Had Harry given her the same costume and sent her up here to punish Natalia for this little act of desperation? How could he do something so awful? So *humiliating*?

Natalia hung from the bar, then leapt to the next, inching closer to the center of the tent. The other woman did the same.

Closer now, Natalia could see that this was not Dorothy. The woman was Natalia.

The other suddenly leapt again, breaking their synchronicity for the first time. Natalia's body filled with dread.

She leapt again and Natalia found herself dangling from the trapeze, high in the air, face to face with her double. Natalia immediately spotted the scar on her double's face - dark and inflamed, as bad as it had been the day of the incident.

The double swung herself hard and kicked Natalia in the legs. Scared and in need of leverage, Natalia wrapped her legs around the bar and pulled herself all the way up to stand, placing all of her weight on her good foot, and carefully turned around, intending to make her way back to the platform and climb back down to safety.

But just as she was about to jump, she felt a heavy thud in the small of her back and Natalia's foot slipped. She kept her grip on the rope with one hand and avoided plummeting to the ground, but unintentionally looked down at the immense space below her - something she never did under normal circumstances, as even an accomplished acrobat such as herself could easily become afraid of falling from such a great height if she allowed herself to think about it.

She looked above her shoulder to see the double stare at her with that devilish, disturbing smile.

Natalia squirmed and repositioned both hands on the bar, then focused on the platform. She swung back and forth with pain radiating from her broken foot through the entire right side of her body, wobbling and clinging to the bar like an amateur, scared and unsure of her own talent.

She needed a moment to steady herself, but there was no time; this thing, whoever or whatever it was, would keep coming after her. It wanted to sabotage her act. It wanted to hurt her.

Natalia made the final jump and nearly cried with relief when she landed on the wooden platform. She longed for nothing more than good night's sleep in her bed and something, anything, to dull the excruciating pain. It was nearly unbearable and it was taking a level of self-restraint Natalia had never known to avoid breaking down in tears in front of a hundred people.

She lowered herself to her knees and gripped the rope ladder with trembling hands. As she began to climb down, she glanced behind her just in time to see the double land on the platform and tower over her.

Slowly, the other woman kneeled down to look her straight in the eyes. They had the same eyes, the brownish grey with the tiny flecks of green. Suddenly, she gripped Natalia's shoulders and shoved her backward. Natalia slipped, but managed to grasp the next rung of the ladder tight enough to keep from falling.

As she dangled from the ladder, her hands chaffing on the course rope, Natalia looked to the ground below her. She could climb down the ladder safely and run back to her bed to enjoy one more night in her wagon before being banished from the circus and replaced with some young ingénue.

Or... she could let go. The frustration of dealing with Harry, the loneliness of constantly moving from town to town with no home or family, and the fear of being left behind... it would end if she just let go.

But she didn't want to let go. She wanted to be here. The trapeze was her home; it certainly didn't belong to this thing that stared down at her now. Fury washed over her and she found a burst of energy that propelled her back up the ladder and onto the platform.

The smug expression fell from the double's face as she was suddenly confronted with Natalia - the real Natalia, the Natalia who knew what she was doing here and was no longer afraid of her or of the great distance beneath them.

Natalia shoved her as hard as she could. Her double pushed off the platform enough to grab onto the first bar. Natalia followed, jumping onto the bar and standing on top of her double's hands as she hung below.

With her stronger foot, she stomped on the double's hand, causing her to jerk away, but not to fall.

Natalia leapt to the next bar and swung with her usual grace. Even with the broken foot, she felt like herself again. Like a professional. Like a hummingbird.

But this hummingbird was going to need to fight.

In a swift motion, Natalia dropped from a standing position on the bar to hanging from it, again bringing them face to face. She gathered all of her momentum to swing hard and kick the double straight in the face with her strong foot.

Now it was the other's turn to flee. She jumped to the platform, barely holding onto it with her fingertips. Natalia felt a rush of adrenaline, emboldened by seeing her rival struggle. She knew the trapeze and could do this with her eyes closed - in fact, she *had* done it with her eyes closed many times before. It was time to do what she came here to do, even with her damaged foot and a broken heart. It was time to finish the act. It was time to shine.

She let go and somersaulted through the air to the next bar, landing with perfect precision.

But as she prepared for her last leap to the platform, the double instead leapt toward her, grabbing onto Natalia's broken foot and hanging from it.

Natalia cried out in pain and kicked her attacker with her stronger foot to no avail. The double smiled again, appearing to take pleasure in the agony it was causing for Natalia.

She began to climb up Natalia's leg as if it were a rope. Natalia squirmed and wiggled and tried to break free, but failed.

She was *heavy*. Natalia could feel herself breaking a sweat, and sweaty palms meant that holding onto the bar would be impossible within the next few seconds. She needed to drop one of her arms in order to push the double away and loosen its grip around her body, but could not trust that she could hold so much weight with only one damp hand.

But she had no other choice. She let go with her right hand and pushed the double's face away from her as hard as she could. The double swayed, fighting to keep her grip around Natalia's body. Natalia pushed her and hit her even harder and the double nearly fell, but grabbed onto Natalia's free hand.

They dangled there together, Natalia posing mid-air, a hummingbird holding the weight of the world on her tiny wing.

Her grip on the bar would not last much longer.

Their eyes met. Natalia saw the scar on the double's face and remembered the little girl back in Siret.

With the last bit of energy Natalia could find within her, she stomped on the other woman's shoulder as hard as she could.

And the double let go.

Time seemed to slow as the woman fell. The farther away she became, the less she appeared to be real. This imposter, this apparition, or whatever dreadful being she was faded into thin air and disappeared entirely before reaching the dirt below.

Natalia gathered her momentum and performed one last somersault from the bar to the safety of the wooden platform.

The audience erupted in rapturous applause.

* * *

The rain cascaded outside.

Natalia emerged from the tent dragging her shattered limb behind her, in so much pain she would have fallen into the mud and crawled back to her wagon had Ida not seen her and come running to prop her up. As soon as they reached her room, she collapsed on the bed, her mind a storm of exhaustion, confusion, and pain, and fainted.

Natalia awoke the next morning to see several of her circus brethren nearby. There was Ida, of course, and also the fire jugglers, Davey and Mikos, and even Belinda the Snake Charmer (without her snakes, to Natalia's relief).

"There she is," said Mikos. "How are you feeling?"

Natalia felt a stabbing pain in the back of her head. She sat up, propping herself up with her pillow, and winced. Ida reached for a nearby pitcher and poured her a glass of ice water.

"Drink up, doll," she said in a concerned but comforting tone. "You must be thirsty. You've been asleep for..." She looked over to Davey, who checked his pocket watch.

"Almost fourteen hours," he answered.

Still dazed, Natalia noticed the cat curled up in a ball beside her.

"That little guy has been with you all night. I think he's looking out for you," said Ida.

Natalia smiled, just a little, and gently scratched its head. The cat purred.

"What happened last night?" Natalia asked, cautiously. She was fairly convinced it had all been a hideous nightmare, but she had never woken from any nightmare feeling as terrible as she felt now.

"Well, none of us were there for your performance, but we saw you stumble out of the tent afterwards, and boy, did you look terrible!" Ida said. "So we knew you'd gone ahead and done the act, even with your broken foot."

Natalia noticed that her foot had been bandaged, wrapped in ice, and propped on a pillow that was not hers. A sudden feeling of warmth came over her. No one had ever done such a thing for her before.

"My, that sure was brave," said Belinda. "I can't even imagine doing what you did in that kind of pain. And I'll tell you something else, that Harry Monroe is a son of a bitch for trying to get rid of you."

"He sure is," Davey agreed. "But don't you worry about that now. We went ahead and took care of it."

Natalia did not quite understand what he meant, but she had a strong feeling that Ida was behind whatever this was.

Sure enough, Ida nodded. "We all told him that if you go, we go."

"Yeah, and not just us," Belinda added. "Igby the dog-faced boy, Irving with the tattoos, and the whole band agreed, too."

Natalia's eyes welled up with tears. She could not find the words to thank them. But she did not need to.

Ida saw her about to cry and wrapped her arms around her. "Don't worry, doll. Everything's going to be just fine. You just need to get some rest now. Let yourself heal. I'll bring you some dinner in a little while."

The group took their leave and Natalia began to sob. Why? She was not entirely sure. She was not going to be replaced. She would not have to start over in a dusty town full of strangers. She was home. And she was going to be all right.

Natalia took in the quiet of the empty room for a moment before noticing that her vanity mirror, the possession she treasured most in the world, had broken in two.

The Immigrant

Philadelphia, PA

1849

O, my Dark Rosaleen,
   Do not sigh, do not weep!
     The priests are on the ocean green,
They march along the deep.
There's wine from the royal Pope,
Upon the ocean green;
And Spanish ale shall give you hope,
My Dark Rosaleen!
My own Rosaleen!
Shall give you health, and help, and hope,
Shall glad your heart, shall give you hope,
My Dark Rosaleen!

Over hills, and thro' dales,
Have I roamed for your sake;
All yesterday I sailed with sails
On river and on lake.
The Erne, at its highest flood,
I dashed across unseen,
For there was lightning in my blood,
My Dark Rosaleen!
My own Rosaleen!
O, there was lightning in my blood,
Red lightning lightened thro' my blood.
My Dark Rosaleen!

All day long, in unrest,
To and fro, do I move.
The very soul within my breast
Is wasted for you, love!
The heart in my bosom faints
To think of you, my Queen,
My life of life, my saint of saints,
My Dark Rosaleen!
My own Rosaleen!
To hear your sweet and sad complaints,
My life, my love, my saint of saints,
My Dark Rosaleen!

Woe and pain, pain and woe,
Are my lot, night and noon,
To see your bright face clouded so,
Like to the mournful moon.
But yet will I rear your throne
Again in golden sheen;
'Tis you shall reign, shall reign alone,
My Dark Rosaleen!

My own Rosaleen!
'Tis you shall have the golden throne,
'Tis you shall reign, and reign alone,
My Dark Rosaleen!
Over dews, over sands,
Will I fly, for your weal:
Your holy delicate white hands
Shall girdle me with steel.
At home, in your emerald bowers,
From morning's dawn till eve,
You'll pray for me, my flower of flowers,
My Dark Rosaleen!

- James Clarence Mangan

The heavy bang of the door as it slammed shut behind her would echo in her mind forever.

*   *   *

Frances woke up in a panic when the pain crashed over her body. She felt as if every bone below her shoulders had shattered at once. Her bed was wet. The bleeding started right away. The baby was coming and there was nothing Frances could do but desperately try to breathe in between screams.

The nosey women from the other flats came right away. Of course they did. They had hovered over her for weeks, pelting her with orders about what to eat, when to sleep, which chores must be done immediately and which were too strenuous for a woman in her condition. Here they were again, unwelcome, but not unexpected.

Thomas made himself scarce. Where he had gone, Frances did not know. The winter wind was still bitter enough to bite through the skin, especially in the middle of the night, but this was a large city full of men who worked at all hours and plenty of pubs stayed open until dawn.

When the door closed behind him, her mind flashed to the door of the ship as she looked out to the crowded docks, wishing her own parents and siblings had been among the weeping families bidding farewell to the loved ones about to sail to the New World.

Frances could not tell what had made her heart ache more: the sight of so many desperate people, starving, weeping, praying for their loved ones to make it out alive while they knew they themselves had no chance of surviving here at home, or the sight of the door slamming shut with her on the other side, its heavy bolt locking her into the ship and sealing her fate.

They had said good-bye to her, of course, but could not bear to go with her to the docks. She thought of her parents, gaunt and pale, huddling in the doorway to their tiny home, relieved to see their now married eldest daughter leaving for what they assumed had to be a better life.

But it wasn't a better life. Not for Frances.

Frances believed in Ireland.

Even when the Great Hunger had reached a crisis and so many of her people perished in the rain and the mud. Even when Father Byrne told them at Mass that they must marry and continue to have babies despite being surrounded by death, and have faith that God would care for them in this time of tragedy. It was the first and only time in Frances's life she had disagreed with him. How dare he expect her to bring a child into the world only to see it starve to death in her arms? As a man of God, he knew nothing of bearing children or of grieving them when they were lost.

And "tragedy" was hardly a strong enough word for how her country suffered.

When Frances managed to unearth the few potatoes that grew under withered leaves on their land, she would cut them open only to find them bleeding a disgusting brown slime. A house that attracted starving dogs to its premises was a tell-tale sign that someone inside had died, and families scrambled to bury their loved ones before the animals could eat what was left of them.

All the while, the British landlords did nothing, the dereliction of their own responsibilities having crossed well into abject cruelty.

Still, she believed that young people such as herself would see their homeland through this terrible time. The grim state of affairs had lead them to delay marriage, as young would-be husbands had nothing to offer a future bride and no prospects to provide for a family. Friends Frances had known since all of them were babies met in one cottage or another, huddled by a small fire, hungry and tired, speaking to one another only in Irish Gaelic, cursing the British for their callousness and imagining a future where the Irish answered to no one but their own.

The hunger pains were unbearable, but the time spent with her dearest friends gave her a reason to rise in the morning. This was especially true for one friend in particular, Lottie Morgan.

The Morgans lived a stone's throw from Frances and her family, and the days spent playing with Lottie in the green pastures beyond her home, when the young girls were inseparable from one another, comprised Frances's earliest memories.

It was Lottie who had first told her about changelings.

In the meadow behind her cottage, Frances saw something she could not explain: a small insect or perhaps even a tiny, baby bird resting on the petals of a flower. Frances stared as it seemed to wake from a nap and hop to the next flower, then the next. Suddenly, it looked at her and realizing it had been seen, darted away from her and quickly disappeared.

"It was a faerie!" Young Lottie exclaimed. "It must have been!"

Young Frances was filled with a sense of wonder for a moment, until Lottie revealed why a faerie would be watching them now: Frances's mother was expecting a new baby.

"The faeries shall be watching you! They want the new baby," she explained as she jumped from one mud puddle to the next, her dark brown ringlets bouncing across the side of her face.

"But why?" Frances demanded, her round eyes growing even wider.

"The faeries bring their own to the human world when it's time for them to die. They take healthy human babies and replace them with a sickly creature so they can rest here forever."

The story terrified young Frances.

Lottie also told her that envying a baby made them especially susceptible to a faerie's power, so Frances vowed to never look upon her new sibling with jealousy. When he was born, she watched over him day and night, convinced faeries would flutter in through the chimney and take him away.

When the baby perished anyway, Frances was inconsolable. It took Mother and Father weeks to convince her that faeries were not real and that sometimes babies just didn't make it through the night. It was sad, but it happened, and most importantly, it was no one's fault.

More siblings came after that, and all of them survived. Now, years later, they indulged Frances as she taught them Gaelic and spoke of Irish independence at home. They sat by the fire at night, singing and reciting poetry in the native Irish tongue.

> *My own Rosaleen,*
> *'Tis you shall have the golden throne,*
> *'Tis you shall reign, and reign alone.*
> *My dark Rosaleen,*
> *Over dews, over sands,*
> *Will I fly, for your weal,*
> *Your holy delicate hands*
> *Shall guide me with steel*
> *At home, in your emerald bowers,*
> *From morning's dawn till eve,*
> *You will pray for me, my flower of flowers,*
> *My dark Rosaleen.*

Frances, Lottie, and their loyal compatriots believed in a future where Ireland would once again see the light break through the dark clouds of the Great Hunger, if only they could hold on a little longer.

Frances's parents did not share that belief.

Thomas Pearce was not a man of means, but he was a hard worker who had saved enough to book passage on a ship to America, and Frances's father convinced him to marry her and bring her along.

Frances was shocked that the decision had been made without her and angered that her father should order her to marry a man she did not know, or at least, she did not know him well. He lived in the same town and worked anywhere he could, but there was nothing remarkable about him, nothing that caused her to remember if she had ever spoken with him before.

She couldn't marry a strange man who meant nothing to her. She couldn't leave her home and her friends. She couldn't leave Lottie.

But the reality of the country's hardship was one that could not be argued. Her parents were desperate to see their child make it out alive. They, like so many others, had begged the moneylenders for help until they lacked both the money to leave and the strength to plead for the mercy of those who could provide it.

As compelled as Frances felt to honor their efforts to protect her, she agreed to it only when Lottie told her to go.

"You have a chance here, Frances. You are of no use to Ireland if you are dead, are you?" said Lottie, and both of their hearts broke in tandem. "Ireland will not love you any less from afar."

Frances and Thomas were married a week later, the very day they were due to set sail. She never did learn why Thomas had agreed to take her, sacrificing more of his savings to pay her way onto the ship as well. She suspected that he didn't want to arrive alone in a new country full of strangers, but never dared to ask him if that were the case.

The boat made her sick. She was very thin by that time, and so, so tired. The storms outside that violently rocked them back and forth made her head spin and her stomach flip, and the small amount of food she had inside her didn't stay there for long.

Frances could hardly tell which made her more ill: the motion of the ship or the smell of her fellow passengers. They were packed together tightly and slept on a thin layer of straw on the cold floor. The water provided was brown and hideous and those who dared to drink it regretted it moments later. Tin buckets of filth piled up around the edges of the room, frequently tipping over when the ship heaved from side to side.

The utter devastation back at home had been more than tragic; it had been exhausting. But as much as Frances wanted to collapse on the cold straw on the floor, she was unable to find much sleep on the journey. When others settled in at night, Frances would instead walk alone on the deck of the ship and gaze at the vast expanse of the stars above her.

The sight was almost enough to allay the heavy sense of what she could only identify as grief; and good cause she had to be in grief, for her life, as she knew it, was behind her now, growing smaller by the moment. Frances thought of Lottie and of all she wanted to do for her fellow Irishmen and wondered how to do anything for them from another world.

Perhaps she could send money so they may stave off the landlords a bit longer. Perhaps she could convince Americans to look with mercy on the plight of Ireland and become allies for their independence. Perhaps, perhaps, perhaps. The grief was palpable. But underneath it was an undeniable sense of hope.

She wasn't rested enough when the ship docked in a large city called Philadelphia, and when the passengers were all herded onto land like cattle, she struggled to stand upright, her mind still tossing and turning with the ocean waves.

The city was loud, crowded, smelled like mold, and looked... ugly. There were no trees or green grass, nothing but bricks and iron and concrete, the sodden streets packed with human cargo as rain poured outside.

Everyone had told her this was a small price to pay for the chance to live free of the deadly hunger she faced every day at home, but here she stood in this disgusting pig pen, still tired, still thirsty, and still hungry.

The tiny flat Thomas had found for them was not a respite from any of the sounds or smells of this New World. It had three rooms, and Thomas insisted they were lucky to have so many, but the walls were thin and the air was cold. Babies cried, children fought, dogs barked, and women chatted with each other outside, lamenting the fact that the rain had soaked the laundry they had hung to dry.

Thomas built a fire in the tiny cast iron stove, then decided it was time for their marriage to be consummated. He had been patient while she had been ill on the boat, but now, he said, he had waited long enough.

* * *

Frances knew as soon as her bleeding stopped that she was with child, and as her belly grew over the months, so did her longing for home. The rainy days finally relented, but with the sunshine came the sweltering summer heat.

It was the kind of heat that made even the most jovial of people angry and shortsighted, though Frances was skeptical that joy was ever something that resided in her corner of this strange city. She learned very quickly that the city was growing faster than it could handle, with dozens of boats of immigrants from all over Europe - indeed, all over the world - arriving every day. Newcomers fought for menial jobs, drank to dull their resentment of one another, and spat venomous insults toward each other in the street.

And though tensions fueled the city from every block and every corner, it was clear to Frances that Irish Catholics were the least welcome of all.

The newspapers were full of hurtful cartoons depicting them as illiterate animals and signs all around the city hung in windows informing them they were not welcome inside. Anywhere she dared to walk beyond her stifling tenement building, Frances felt exposed. Her peach-colored hair and freckles gave her away as Irish, and though there were plenty of Scotch-Irish citizens in the city, most of whom had been there for generations already, shopkeepers tended to err on the side of assuming, correctly, that she was a part of this massive wave of Irish Catholic refugees who had fled starvation, endured the ship from Hell, and landed here only to be treated like a rabid dog.

But as homesick as Frances frequently felt, she couldn't deny the most important need of their journey to America had been met: America had food.

Thomas had, thankfully, found a job laboring over the new railroad for the state of Pennsylvania. It was hard, backbreaking work done over long hours of the day, and he usually came home sweaty, sunburned, and too tired for any relations with Frances, which suited her just fine. Thomas barely earned enough to afford the roof over their heads, but the days in which Frances went hungry had now become the exception and not the bitter, painful rule.

Thomas also had a terrible cough that never seemed to go away. He'd had it on the ship, but the ship was so dank and disgusting, it was impossible not to fall ill, so Frances ignored it when she could. But it seemed to grow worse now, and it annoyed her at night when she tried to sleep beside him.

The longer she lived with Thomas, the more her indifference to him morphed into a kind of sympathy for the damage this work was clearly doing to his body, so Frances cooked for him and made him tea, otherwise keeping their interactions as simple as possible.

It didn't take long for the other women in the building to identify the new girl and for them to assume she needed an overwhelming amount of advice.

At first, Frances kept to herself in her flat to avoid them, but it really didn't matter. Most of them came over uninvited when they felt like it, anyway. When the summer heat finally relented and a cool autumn breeze drifted over the river and into the neighborhood, Frances spent more of her time in the courtyard outside while the women all washed their clothes and hung them to dry.

From the narrow wooden steps where she sat, belly swollen and back aching from the extra weight in her body, she could see the skyline over the river, dotted with trees whose leaves turned to lovely shades of gold and red, and even Frances had to admit that the warm colors against the brown and grey buildings was a sight of beauty.

"Do you need anything, my dear?" asked Mrs. O'Riordan, a woman of middle age who seemed to have appointed herself the matriarch of the small tenement community. "Bring us some of your clothes to wash. We won't mind a few extra things."

"Oh, come now, Annie," said Mrs. Lynn. "She is not completely helpless, is she?" Mrs. Lynn was a younger mother with three girls whose names Frances did not bother to remember.

"Best to keep an eye on expectant mums," Mrs. O'Riordan replied. "We don't need the faeries paying a visit, now do we?"

Of all the things Frances missed about home, and there certainly were many, childhood superstitions had not made their way onto that list.

But Mrs. O'Riordan's mention of faeries made her think of Lottie.

They had written to each other several times over the months, though the letters were slow to travel such a great distance between them. Frances kept the most recent one in the pocket of her apron, and having been reminded of it, reached for it to read it yet again.

Dear Frances,

    How often it is that I think of you and wish you were here with us, but I remind myself, over and over, that it is best you are not. We had hoped for more to harvest this year, but the rot has spared none of our crops, and conditions continue to be poor. It has rained a great deal lately, and the dreary weather has kept many of us in bed for much of our days. The hunger makes it difficult to sleep at night, and I find myself feeling hopelessly tired. I wish only wonderful things for you, Frances, and my relief knowing you are in a better world eases the longing I feel for your company. I am happy for you, but remember fondly that Ireland was better off with you in it.

All my love,
Lottie

Somehow, Lottie's description of how tired they felt made Frances tired, too, and a sinking feeling came over her. It wasn't merely a feeling of homesickness this time. Now, it was tainted with guilt. Here she sat, married, pregnant, and recently fed a breakfast of apples and fresh bread, far from her loved ones and unable to aid them in their cause.

A part of her wanted to cry. A part of her wanted to sleep. But the greatest urge of all pushed her to go for a walk to St. Mary's.

Mass had been the one bright spot in Frances's life over the past seven months. Sundays were spent with other refugees like her, all of them scared yet hopeful, weary yet ambitious, weak yet building the strength to start again.

The cathedral was stunning. A massive red building with two stories of meticulously painted stained glass, dark wooden pews, and a painting of Jesus looking down upon his flock as though he were watching over them from Heaven. Back home, their church had been a modest wooden building barely large enough for its congregation - and as the Great Hunger raged, the pews were never empty, as the entire town constantly prayed for a miracle to save them.

She also loved Father Doyle. He was the youngest priest she had ever met and he spoke to them in a gentile voice filled with a tender optimism for their future. He didn't boss them around or speak from a place of righteous conviction for what God wanted her to do or not to do. He spoke of kindness, of family, and of faith that the Hell they lived through in the present would be behind them as they prepared to someday enter the Kingdom of Heaven.

Frances took her place in a pew at the front of the church just as Father Doyle emerged from the rectory.

"Good day to you, Mrs. Pearce," he said to her in his American accent. Frances was impressed that he remembered her name, as they had spoken only a few times after Mass, and only for a second or two.

"Good day, Father."

"And how are you this morning?"

Frances was not expecting to be caught off guard by such a simple question, nor to feel her eyes fill with tears so quickly.

"Oh, dear. What is the matter?"

She shook her head. "I... I do not know."

"May I sit with you?" He asked, respectfully. She nodded and he joined her on the bench beneath the large portrait.

"I want to be grateful, Father, to be alive and to have a place to live and supper to eat nearly every night. I want to be happy. I want it more than anything. But I can't."

He produced a handkerchief from his black robe and handed it to her.

"I did not know what to expect from this world, but I did not expect this. The noise and the smells... the cruelty coming from half the city... it hurts as much as the hunger hurt back home. The love I had in times gone by that has since been lost to me is all I can think of, and I cannot bear it."

Father Doyle nodded. "We live in a very painful time on this Earth, Mrs. Pearce. Sometimes we must accept that our souls will hurt, and we must allow ourselves to grieve what has been lost to us."

A part of her had been expecting to be shamed for how she felt and told to focus on God's plan for her and her child, or assailed with more advice for which she had not asked. But Father Doyle just listened.

"How do you live with it, Father? The suffering, the injustice? How do you hold onto your faith in a world so awful as this one?"

"A reasonable question," he said, smiling just a little. "I don't suppose you are aware that this is my second church?"

She shook her head.

"My prior congregation gathered at St. Augustine, not terribly far from here. A few years ago, it was burned to the ground in a horrible riot."

"By whom?"

"A group of angry Protestants."

Her heart sank. "And what did you do?"

"I thanked God that no one was seriously harmed, I forgave the men responsible, and I came to St. Mary's to begin anew."

"And what of your anger? Where does it go?"

"You must understand, many people in this country fled tyranny imposed onto them by the Church, and indeed by the Pope himself. We do our best to act on the will of God, but no man is infallible, and we Catholics have caused pain as often as we have endured it at the hands of others."

He took both of her hands in his. "Anger, like grief, can turn into despair if we allow it. Do not allow yourself to fall into such despair, Mrs. Pearce. Look for ways to love your fellow man instead."

Nothing had made her feel so comforted since before the Great Hunger began. The tears on her cheeks had dried, and Father Doyle's soft hands wrapped around hers made her feel as though angels were near.

"Frances," she told him. "Please. Call me Frances."

He smiled. "That is a lovely name. It means 'free,' does it not?"

"Oh, I... I am afraid I do not know. I was named for my mother's mother. She passed before I was born."

"I see," Father Doyle said. "That must also be a heavy weight to bear."

"What?"

"Your name, which means 'free,' has tied you to the concept of death since the day you were born."

She had never thought of it in this way, but when he said the words aloud, she felt as though he saw her in a way that most others never had.

"But that can be a beautiful thing," he said. "For death, and the entrance into Heaven, will someday free us from the suffering of this world. In the meantime, Frances, we were put here on Earth to forgive one another. Find it in your heart to love as best you can."

That night, Frances wrote to Lottie as she waited for Thomas to come home.

My dear Lottie,

I wish, more than anything, that I could be as strong as you want me to be and to tell you of the wonderful life I have embraced here in Philadelphia. Alas, the truth is more complicated. My gratitude for all that I have is tainted by my desire to be with you. My body is here, but my heart still lies across the sea. I love my country and believe in the strength of her spirit to rise above the anguish that plagues her, but most of all, I love and believe in you. It is my greatest wish to see you again someday, though I fear it may not be in this life and we must find each other in the next. Only then will I be reunited with my own heart, and only then will I feel complete once more.

All my love,
Frances

* * *

The winter months were more difficult than Frances had imagined. The harsh wind whipped straight across the building from the icy river. The cost of food rose as fishermen were not able to catch fish through the frozen waters, and Thomas, as removed as he often was from their life in the flat, had correctly prioritized food for his pregnant wife over coal for the stove.

And of course, the nosey neighbors continued to buzz about.

Mrs. O'Riordan was perhaps the most annoying. Two of her children had grown and married, and the other two, both boys in their teenage years, worked outside of the home as bricklayers with Mr. O'Riordan, leaving her with little else to do during the day but fuss over Frances and her growing belly.

What bothered Frances the most, however, was the fact that Mrs. O'Riordan was the most superstitious of the small community and often referenced the faeries and their supposed plot to steal Frances's baby.

Mother had told her, over and over again, that faeries were not real, but Frances was never entirely convinced. The timing of her brother's death in relation to her apparent sighting of one in the meadow seemed to be too much of a coincidence.

The sight of his little blue face in the cradle that morning haunted her memories, and the mere thought of the same thing happening to her own child filled her with a kind of dread so crippling, she blocked the thought of impending motherhood from her mind completely.

Unless, of course, Mrs. O'Riordan was nearby.

"You mustn't forget to breathe, that is the most important thing of all," she instructed. "Don't squeeze your eyes shut or they will turn red and stay that way for months. A bath may make the child come quicker, but I'm afraid it will be too cold to bring you outside."

Frances rubbed a painful spot on the lower part of her back.

"And once the babe has arrived, remember to keep tending to your husband. It's easy to forget them, I'm afraid, but a wife mustn't neglect to be a wife even after she has also become a mother."

Frances knew this, but still struggled to think of Thomas as more important than a helpless infant.

"And keep a fire going at all times. Not only is the cold bad for the child, but it will deter the wee folk from coming into your home."

With that, Frances found herself in need of fresh air and announced she would go to check for the daily post, hoping to hear from Lottie.

But there was nothing, and Frances began to worry. She had not heard from her in weeks. Surely, if something terrible had happened to her, Mother and Father would have written to tell her... unless the same fate had descended upon them, too. As far as Frances knew, the Hunger had not improved since she had set sail for America, and if Ireland's fortune did not turn in the spring, there would soon be nothing left.

That night, Frances dreamed of cutting potatoes back home with a small knife, causing them to bleed. It wasn't just the hideous slime that had come from them when the disease first infected their land, but worse somehow. Thicker. Darker. It was human blood that dripped from inside. She grabbed another, and another, and another, blood oozing from each and every one, until her hands and dress were soaked.

From behind her, a baby cried, and Frances turned just in time to see the faeries carry it with them up the chimney.

Then, there was the pain.

* * *

It lasted all through the day and into the following night. The women took turns staying with her, cleaning the soiled floors and sheets and wiping the sweat from her feverish forehead.

Delirious, Frances begged them to open the windows and let in the cold winter air, and even though the other women bundled up in wool shawls, her skin still burned underneath her nightdress.

> *All day long, in unrest,*
> *To and fro, do I move.*
> *The very soul within my breast*
> *Is wasted here for you...*

She mumbled the poem as a way to remind herself that she was still awake.

The room blurred in front of her exhausted eyes, and for a moment, the lamplight seemed to flicker and swirl around the room. She stared ahead and a strange sight took shape before her eyes: a cluster of little balls of light seemed to be dancing near the stove.

"Stay with us, dear," said Mrs. O'Riordan. "It won't be long now. Just breathe."

Frances was suddenly overcome with an urge to run. But even if there had been anywhere to run to, she couldn't possibly move; the pain anchored her to the floor and she hadn't the strength to push past the women who hovered over her.

> *The heart in my bosom faints*
> *To think of you, my Queen,*
> *My life of life, my saint of saints,*
> *My dark Rosaleen.*

A surge of pressure bore down on her entire body and Frances cried out in pain.

"This is it," Mrs. Lynn told her. "Be brave, Frances, you're almost there. Just push."

Mrs. Lynn held onto her forearms as Frances closed her eyes and did as she was instructed.

She felt the baby finally drop from her body, then immediately fainted.

* * *

Frances woke hours later, overheating in her bed. The sheets had been changed. The room was quiet. And next to her in her bed, tightly wrapped in a tiny blanket, was her baby, sound asleep.

It was dark in the flat, save for a small glow of a lamplight coming from the main room.

The lower half of her body felt as though it had been ripped apart. Uneasy on her feet, Frances made her way to the door and opened it, peering out of the darkness, and squinted at the small bit of orange light.

Mrs. O'Riordan sat in a wooden chair across from Thomas.

"Look who's awake!" she exclaimed upon seeing Frances. "Come, dear, come sit down," she said, standing and gesturing for Frances to take her place. Then, her brow furrowed. "Where is he?"

Frances felt confused. Where was who?

"Oh, you poor thing, you must be in so much pain. Come and sit, I will fetch the boy."

The boy. She had given birth to a son.

She slowly stepped across the room. For the first time, she noticed that someone - presumably Mrs. O'Riordan - had filled her bloomers with a cool, damp towel. It helped ease the pain a little as she lowered herself onto the chair.

Thomas gave her a look, but said nothing. Frances could not peg what he was thinking at first, but he didn't appear to be unhappy or even as stoic as he typically was. He wasn't smiling, but something in his face told her that he was pleased. He reached for her hand and gave it an affectionate squeeze. Then, startling her, he pulled away and coughed loudly for a few seconds.

Mrs. O'Riordan emerged with the little bundle. "Here we are, daddy," she said to Thomas, placing the child in his arms. "What are you two going to name the wee thing?"

Oh, a name. Frances had expected to name a girl after her mother, as was tradition in her family, but hadn't even thought of a name for a boy. The pressure of the decision suddenly overwhelmed her and her mind seemed to forget every boy's name she had ever heard in her life.

Thomas looked at her, expecting an answer, but nothing came.

"Thomas," he finally said. "We'll call him Thomas Franklin

Pearce, Jr."

Frances wasn't sure how to feel about Thomas naming the child after himself, but once the words had been spoken, Thomas looked at the baby and smiled for the first time, so Frances decided then to keep any objection to herself.

A coughing fit suddenly came over Thomas again. He thrust the baby toward Frances, who now found herself holding her child for the very first time. He seemed peaceful at first, but in a second, his tiny red face twisted and he began to cry.

Frances shot a concerned look to Mrs. O'Riordan.

"Oh, you will have to get used to that noise, I'm afraid," the older woman told her. "You will hear it often from now on."

Frances was unsure of what to do. She slowly rocked back and forth to try and soothe him, but it didn't seem to be working.

Still in the midst of his coughing fit, Thomas stood up and stepped outside into the cold to excuse himself.

"Shall I leave you be then, Mrs. Pearce?" Mrs. O'Riordan asked. "It's probably best for the three of you to get some sleep."

"All right," Frances said. Rest was something she wanted, but a part of her suddenly didn't want Mrs. O'Riordan to go.

Mrs. O'Riordan surprised her by leaning down to kiss Frances on the head. "Don't worry so much, dear. 'Tis the most natural thing in the world for women to become mothers."

As Frances looked down at her screaming baby, she hoped to God that would turn out to be true.

* * *

The weeks that followed were a blur of screaming, rocking, nursing, and frustrated sighs coming from Thomas, who didn't understand why she couldn't keep the baby quiet at night while he tried to sleep.

Frances began to wish that Thomas would not come home after work; that he would instead find a pub and drink with his friends, as he sometimes did at the end of the week, and leave her alone to handle her child without having to worry about her husband as well.

One night, perhaps a month after the baby was born, Frances got her wish.

She was relieved, at first, when Thomas hadn't come home at

his usual time and figured he would stumble in drunk, sleep soundly for a few hours, and not be bothered if the baby cried before the dawn. But as she prepared to sleep that night, a man came to tell her that Thomas had fallen ill while working outside, collapsed during a coughing fit, and never stood up again.

Frances knew that she should have felt pity for Thomas, a hard-working man who had done nothing but work himself to the bone since they had arrived in Philadelphia and did not deserve to meet such a fate. Or she should have felt fear for what would happen to her and her baby without his money. Instead, she simply thought of home and longed to return to Ireland now that the shackles of being married to Thomas had been lifted.

But she knew in her heart there was no choice to be made. The letters from home had stopped and Frances had a strong idea as to why. She also doubted that she or her infant son would even survive the boat ride back across the Atlantic.

The baby slept quietly in the tiny wooden cradle Mrs. Lynn had given her since her youngest had outgrown it, and Frances sat in the dark, alone.

> *To hear your sweet and sad complaints,*
> *My life, my love, my saint of saints,*
> *My dark Rosaleen...*

She stared at nothing for hours until the baby woke and began to cough. It was a rattling sound that came from deep in his tiny lungs. She finally broke her gaze and peered into the cradle at him. The noise did not relent and became a hideous mixture of coughing and screaming.

A tiny glimmer of light near the stove caught her eye, but when she turned her head to get a proper look, it was gone.

She looked back at the cradle and a sinking feeling came over her.

This sickly creature was not her son.

* * *

Frances considered telling Mrs. O'Riordan of this discovery, as her superstitious nature was bound to make her believe it, but she feared what Mrs. O'Riordan would do. She would tell the other wives and they would blame Frances for failing to protect her baby, and even though Frances did not particularly like these women or want to be a part of their myopic lives inside the walls of this building, being cast out of the circle would leave her with nothing.

She decided instead to visit Father Doyle.

The sun had barely begun to shine on the red brick when she came knocking on the large wooden doors. He did not answer. Rather than bring the changeling back to her home, she sat outside and waited in the cold until he arrived, her breath hanging in the air and her feet cold in the snow.

She would have fallen asleep leaning against the wall if the changeling had not been coughing and crying the entire time.

"Frances?" She finally heard him say as he approached the church to open it for the day. "What on earth is the matter? You must be freezing."

It was only when he removed his wool coat and wrapped it around her and the changeling that she realized she had not even gotten dressed before leaving the flat and still wore her nightgown with no shawl or blanket.

He ushered her inside.

"What troubles you? Has something happened?"

She looked down at the baby. "Father, I must tell you something, and it is something you will not want to hear. But for the love of God, I need you to believe me. This is not my child."

She handed the baby to him. Though caught by surprise, Father Doyle took him and cradled the crying monster in his arms.

"It is a changeling. I saw the faeries in my home the night he was born, waiting for him, and I swear one came back early this morning to check on him."

"Frances, perhaps you had better sit down—"

"'Twas a faerie theft Father, I swear it is true. I don't know what this thing is or where they have taken my son. I need your help to get him back. I need God's help to make this right."

Father Doyle frowned and cautiously placed the back of his hand on her forehead.

"Are you ill, Mrs. Pearce?"

"No. But that one is," she answered, gesturing to the child.

"It is not uncommon for babies to be sick, especially in the winter months. He just needs to be cared for, that is all." He handed the baby back to Frances and the coughing continued. "Shall I send for Mr. Pearce to bring you home?"

"Thomas is dead. A man came to tell me last night."

Father Doyle sighed heavily. "Oh, dear. That's what this is about, then. I am so very sorry for your loss, Mrs. Pearce. Would you like to pray with me?"

Frances nodded, not just because she needed a moment to speak to God, but because she wanted the kind priest to hold her hand, which he did.

"Mother Mary," he began in his soothing voice, "Please watch over Frances Pearce and her newborn child in this time of loss. Bestow your grace upon them to see them through this hour of darkness and into your divine light. Pray for us now, in the hour of our birth, in the time of our grief, and at the hour of our death, for it is in dying that we are born to eternal life. Amen."

They took a long moment of silence after Father Doyle's prayer, but Frances felt nothing. God was not here in the church with her today. A small part of her wondered if He had ever been.

Frances walked home in Father Doyle's wool coat, which he insisted she keep, and left it on for the rest of the day. Thomas had not recently brought home any coal, and the flat was nearly as cold inside as it was outside.

She crawled under the blankets in her bed and untied her nightdress to feed the baby. As he nursed, she pushed herself to believe what Father Doyle had said; that babies fell ill all the time, and there was nothing unusual about his condition; that Thomas's death had shocked her and caused her to imagine things that were not real; that all she needed was rest.

But sleep never came, at least not for Frances. The baby slept after he nursed, so soundly in fact that Frances could not tell for a moment whether or not he was breathing. The more she stared into his tiny face, the more convinced she became that he was not fated to last through another night. He was a sick creature who had been brought here to die in the human world, and that meant that her real baby was out there, somewhere, among the spirits.

She could keep this weakling in her home and let it pass away, but the sorrow of knowing her own child was lost to her was more than she could bear.

Still wrapped in Father Doyle's coat, she set out to find the creatures responsible for this devilish exchange and make it right.

* * *

The winter sun had already begun to set behind the tall buildings as Frances walked through the city with the sleeping changeling. She worried it might die before she reached the faeries - if indeed she ever reached them at all - and if that were to be the case, they would put up an even bigger fight to keep her real baby for themselves.

Heavy clouds had rolled in and thick snowflakes drifted from high above her as she walked. And walked. And walked.

Frances had done very little in the way of exploring Philadelphia and quickly lost her sense of direction, but it didn't matter. She left it to God to guide her out of the city and into the woods, where the creatures in question were likely to be hiding.

Eventually, the steel and concrete buildings met the forest of bare trees, and any warmth coming from the cobblestones beneath her feet gave way to the icy ground underneath the soft snow.

She came upon a small creek, its tiny veins of water still flowing underneath the thin layer of ice, and carefully stepped on the slippery rocks. She nearly dropped the changeling into the water when she slipped, barely catching herself in time.

It fussed for the first time in hours, no doubt feeling the cold wind on its face and wanting to go home.

"I am trying to bring you home," she said to the changeling. "Be patient and do not let go yet, not until you are back with your own kind."

It cried, ignoring her instruction, and Frances continued to walk.

The forest was quiet. A kind of quiet Frances had never heard before. The moonlight through the clouds cast a silver glow all around her, and Frances longed to rest here in the tall, purple shadows the trees.

The exhaustion finally washed over her and she fell to her knees, consumed with hopelessness. The changeling would not last much longer in the cold, and perhaps she wouldn't, either. If the changeling was going to die, and if her baby were to be lost to her forever, then she may as well lay here in the snow and let herself die, too. She had no home, no family, and no means of survival without Thomas. All that was left for her was sleep.

And though the cold bit through her skin, she could not have asked for a more peaceful resting place.

Just before she shut her eyes, Frances noticed something in the distance: a tiny flicker of light, just as she had seen near the stove in her flat the night the faeries had come for her child.

She sat up quickly and looked ahead. A moment passed and Frances held her breath. But then she saw another, then another.

The changeling coughed and squirmed, unhappy in the cold, but the movement meant the thing was still alive, and Frances was mere moments away from returning it to its rightful place.

She leapt to her feet and followed the little balls of light, but a moment later, they were gone. She looked around in the dark, lost and confused, afraid she had only been imagining what she so desperately wanted to see, until she heard the sound of a baby's cry.

Frances slowly turned to see a large clearing behind her. In the center, wrapped in a wool blanket and placed on a bed of twigs, was a chubby-cheeked human child. The balls of light fluttered around it and Frances's eyes filled with tears.

She walked up to the child and fell to her knees, placing the changeling on the twigs beside him. Her son was heavier than the sick one, clearly healthier, and he looked up at her with wide, blue eyes.

A strong feeling of a love filled her chest as she peered into his beautiful face.

"Hello, my darling," she said to him as she lay down in the snow and wrapped her arms around him.

The changeling continued to cough, but her baby hardly made a sound, save for a few high-pitched coos as his mother held him and a large snowflake landed on his nose.

Her eyelids grew heavy. Frances would need time to gather her strength for the journey back home. For this moment, the best thing she could do for her child was to sing.

Woe and pain, pain and woe,
Are my lot, night and noon,
To see your bright face clouded so,
Like to the mournful moon.
But yet will I rear your throne
Again in golden sheen;
'Tis you shall reign, shall reign alone,
My Dark Rosaleen.

Among the faeries and the white blanket of snow, Frances finally slept.

The Lumberjack

Puget Sound, WA

1861

The fog was particularly heavy that day.

Frederick was new to the Washington logging industry, and the work was hard, but the land was breathtaking. He walked alone through the forest in search of a quiet moment at the nearby river, just outside the bustling mill town where dozens of men lived, worked, ate, drank, fought, and slept.

Frederick had worked his way north since his birth in Missouri some twenty-five years ago, a free man of color, but too close to the South for comfort. When his mother passed and his siblings had married and had families of their own, Frederick felt compelled to move north, as far north as he could, figuring he'd feel safer beyond the border, should he be lucky enough to make it there.

He found farm work in Iowa and Minnesota, then rail yard work in Nebraska, then heard about a booming industry all the way out on the western coast, and figuring it would be in his best interest to make some more money while he was young, traveled out west to find the work and keep close to the border so he could cross it as soon as he felt he could.

It was easy to find a job seeing as how the logging companies needed as many strong men as they could find to take down trees of this size. They were far more massive than anything Frederick had imagined. It took a whole crew of men to pull a tree down, strip the bark from the logs, cut it up into suitable lumber, yard them down to the water, load them all onto rafts to haul down to the mills, saw them up into pieces and only then ship them down the coast to California, where there was plenty of money for the beneficiaries of the so-called California Gold Rush to order more and more and more and more of it.

So here Frederick found himself, trudging through the mud that could get to be knee-deep through the trees that nearly touched the grey sky, and it was at the river that day that he met her.

She was a Native woman who lived nearby with the rest of her tribe, who often came down to the water to trap salmon, and who was familiar, though not friendly, with some of the men who came and went from the mill town near her home. But she didn't know him, and in a rare moment of extroversion, decided to tell him her name, Aponi.

"It's beautiful," he said with the deepest sincerity, refraining to add that she herself was every bit as beautiful as her name, even though he wanted to.

She lifted the basket full of fish to her hip with no effort at all. "Who are you?" she asked, and Frederick realized he'd be too distracted by the sound of her name to give his own.

"My name is Frederick. I'm very pleased to meet you."

"You are a logger?" She asked, and he nodded. "How did you find yourself here?"

"I arrived a few months ago and went to inquire for a job. The boss asked me my name and I told him. He asked, 'What's your last name?' and I said I don't have one. He asked how that could be, but I didn't feel particularly inclined to tell the man I have one all right, I just don't like to use it because it wasn't mine to begin with. Some old white man had given it to some of my kin, who then passed it along to me. He didn't know us and as far as I was concerned, I didn't need to go about introducing myself by the name of a man I will hate until the day I die. So I answered him with nothing more than a shrug. He blinked at me while he decided whether or not to argue and he chose not to. Last name or no last name, he hired me on the spot."

It was the first time he had told anyone those details about himself. It was the first time anyone had asked.

"And here you are," she said, concluding his story for him.

"And here I am."

Her smile felt to him like the sun had finally appeared over the dark clouds after weeks of heavy rain. He could tell that she was like him in a way, that she also observed all that was going on around her with a kind eye and chose not to speak too much, simply because most words didn't always need to be said, and above all, because she enjoyed the quiet.

Frederick enjoyed the quiet, too. The work he had done throughout his life usually involved large teams of men and plenty of noise, especially now that he was logging up in the northwest, and that was acceptable to him because it had to be. Sometimes he would join his fellow workers at the tavern after a long day, but more often than not, he chose to sit alone and admire this beautiful corner of the world where the trees and the sky and the ocean all met and the air smelled of salt and the cool mist of rain washed the sweat off of his forehead.

He hadn't intended to stay here for very long, but the idea of staying put had occurred to him once he realized he found a certain peacefulness in the fortress of the Washington woods.

And when he met her, the decision was set. The border was close if he ever changed his mind, but she had people here and didn't want to leave, and Frederick respected that.

He knew it the first day they spoke by the river, that the peace he felt with her was something special. That she was something special. That she would be worth sticking around for even if he didn't like it here, which fortunately, he did.

Months later, she told him that soon, their roots would grow deeper. Soon, they would be a family.

Then there was a tiny boy who reached for him and smiled and giggled every night when he came home to the cabin they shared, who fell asleep in his arms in the rocking chair he made for him out of excess wood from the job site, and who slowly learned to call him Daddy. Frederick's love for all of it grew deeper by the day as he watched her care for their son. Her family accepted him as one of their own, and even on the tough days when his work had left him battered and exhausted, he knew what awaited him every night when the sun set over the sea. He knew he was home.

*   *   *

Three years had passed since Moses was born. They named him after a man Frederick had never met, but had heard of many times in his home county: George Moses Horton, the Black Bard of North Carolina as he was called, a poet who had published a number of works even though he lived in slavery. The circle of life had long ago decided that a father could not live to care for his son forever, and in a world dominated by white men with money, his son needed to grow up brave like the Bard. But for now, the boy was little, and need not be concerned with the injustices of the world. Frederick would shoulder that burden for him as long as he could.

Bobby was the one who told him about the war. He was a man about Frederick's age who worked along side him, and though Frederick was not generally the talkative type, he enjoyed Bobby's company more than most. He was funny, but not in the way that felt desperate for attention. He was the kind of man who made every person feel like they had a special rapport with him, inside jokes and banter that made the heavy workload feel just a little bit lighter.

And then came the news about the war. Until then, it had been easy - or at least, easier - for Frederick to keep to himself and not think about the atrocities in the South, but now a nervousness possessed the back of his mind every day. If the South won, that would be that. The North would not try again, and slavery would forever be the law of the land.

Bobby must have seen it in Frederick's face, because without a hint of humor, Bobby leaned into him and said, "the North will persevere, I do believe it. And if they don't, Southern men won't come as far as here. And if they try, we'll take care of it right quick." Then the workday went on, like always.

Today, the men needed to find a new spar tree to attach the intricate web of ropes and steel pulleys used to move the heavy lumber from one spot to another.

Ezra was the climber this time, and after a quick inspection of the base to be sure the tree was sturdy enough, Ezra climbed all the way up with a saw in his hand and got to work on cutting off the limbs at the top of the tree.

Frederick hated watching the climbers, but he couldn't help himself. The sight of them so high up in the air made his insides churn, but he had to watch to make sure they were doing OK - and to keep an eye out for himself, since standing at the base of the tree wasn't much safer. The falling branches were called widowmakers for darn good reason.

He tried to think of something else besides Ezra's place atop a forty-foot Douglas fir or the war that ripped through half the country. His gaze drifted out over the magnificent woods. The clouds were starting to part and a little bit of sunlight began to shine through. The trees were never so beautiful as they were when the blue sky surrounded them.

A loud cracking noise jolted Frederick back to the moment, followed by a horrifying scream; a good third of the tree had broken off at the top and came tumbling down with Ezra still holding tightly to it, and it was falling straight toward Frederick.

Frederick leapt out of the way at the last possible second, and both the tree and Ezra hit the earth so hard Frederick was sure the men could feel the tremor all over the mill town. He looked up at the tree to see that the inside was black with rot. Their inspection had been a failure, and without even having to look at the man's broken body beside him, Frederick knew that failure had cost Ezra his life.

As his heart beat in his throat, he thought nothing of the crippling pain that had almost afflicted his body and only of the split second decision that stood between this tree and a lifetime of poverty for Aponi and their son. It was tragic to see a fellow man perish so brutally, but it was not uncommon. Logging was dangerous work and everybody knew it. But if they wanted to make a living, it was a risk they all had to take. All they could do about it was promise to take care of each other's wives if an accident should claim their lives someday.

A drink at the local watering hole followed the day's tragedy. Frederick usually preferred to go home to his family and avoid the drinking, gambling, and inevitable fighting that always seemed to happen there, but tonight was different. It was a break from the usual rowdiness, a show of solidarity and respect for a fellow working man that Frederick hoped would be shown to him if the day ever came.

Bobby was close to Ezra, closer than he was to Frederick or anyone else, so Bobby volunteered to tell Ezra's widow and no one argued. Bad news just didn't feel as upsetting when it came from a man like him, with his unreasonable optimism and his way of looking straight into a person's eyes and making them feel as though they were the only thing in the world that mattered at this moment. But after today, Frederick reckoned that the usually jovial man wouldn't be the same.

It was dark by the time Frederick walked home through the woods. The summer waned. Soon the sun would set before the day's work was even done, and the moisture in the air would find a way to creep under his clothes and freeze him from the inside out.

Their cabin was at the very end of a long line of wooden homes for the loggers, the farthest from the job site and closest to the forest beyond it. Some nights, Frederick walked the long way around rather than pass by everyone else's homes, preferring the crunch of dried mud to any accidental eye contact with his neighbors. Figuring he had spent enough time with them today, he took the scenic route, walking behind the cluster of cabins rather than through it.

It was darker tonight than he had thought, though. It wasn't too cloudy, but a new moon meant no light shone from the sky to show him the path.

It didn't matter; he knew the way and was close enough to the cabins to see the faintest bit of lantern light burn through their windows.

A noise from the forest stopped him. He was no stranger to animals in the woods, but this noise was *loud*. A heavy grunt followed by a deep growl - and it was close, far too close for comfort. Too close to outrun it if he had to.

Frederick slowly turned to face the aggressor, and there a bear stood, staring at him. He froze, barely even allowing his eyes to move as he scanned his surroundings. The most important thing was to make sure there were no cubs nearby, since nothing would make a mama bear feel more threatened than the thought of her cubs in danger. Frederick could certainly relate to and respect that fear.

Sure enough, he could just make out the shape of a bear cub at the base of a tree, only the cub wasn't moving. It appeared to be dead. The mama bear looked at him with heavy eyes and seemed sad, but at the same time, she was out for blood.

Whether the cub's death had anything to do with Frederick or not, he still might pay the price for it if the bear decided to attack. He took a tiny step back and the bear grunted. He took one more and she let out a low growl, a warning for him to stop moving, or else.

"Your heart."

Frederick could hardly tell if someone had whispered it right in his ear or if the wind was playing a dirty trick on his mind.

"Hungry."

It wasn't a word so much as a feeling. His heart beat faster behind his ribs, and though it was as dark as it ever could be in the woods, a part of him somehow felt exposed.

Frederick stood there, frozen, eyes locked with the bear, doing his best to tell it without words that he was not a threat and that she simply needed to go about her business and everything would be just fine.

He was ready to run if he needed, he was ready to calmly back away if he needed, but he was not ready for a piercing shriek that came from the depths of the forest. His hands reflexively flew to his ears to cover them. The bear darted back into the woods, but the shriek came again, immediately followed by a cry of pain coming from the animal and the gut-wrenching noise of bones breaking.

Blood splattered across Frederick's face and chest and dotted the ground all around him as though something had shaken the bear as hard as a wild dog would shake a dead raccoon. He could scarcely see a thing, but knew all he needed to know: whatever that creature was, it was hungry, and he wasn't about to stick around to be dessert.

*   *   *

The next day was a rough one at the camp. The rain came down hard all day long, the men were still shaken by the accident the day before, and to top it off, Bobby had not been heard from since he went to deliver the sad news to Ezra's widow.

Frederick's mind leapt to the worse case, that perhaps Bobby had found himself in the same path he had in front of that awful thing in the woods, but he kept his thoughts to himself lest he cause a stir for no reason. Bobby was probably just sick at home or sleeping late after having a few beers at the dead man's memorial. No one would benefit from worry just for worry's sake, so Frederick thought it best to focus on the day's work and leave it at that.

He took a moment to inspect the broken tree that had taken Ezra's life. The black rot had nearly consumed the whole thing from the inside out, and all that hard work, and even losing Ezra, was worth nothing at the end of the day. Without having time to mourn, the men needed to start over again with a different spar tree, and some other poor climber would have to get up there and perform the tasks that had proved fatal for one of their own the day before.

This time, the climber was a man who went by the name of Brisbee. Frederick didn't know him well, but he worried for the man all the same and could barely bring himself to look as Brisbee climbed.

Frederick and a few others cleared the widowmakers as they landed in the mud and laid out yards and yards of rope to tie around the spar tree, then prepared to lay out the planks for a skid road to help the oxen drag the logs down the hill. It was light work compared to bucking a fallen tree, as he usually did, but the work wore him out all the same.

Exhausted, Frederick trudged home in the thick mud that splashed all the way up to his chest, and he was reminded of the blood that had splattered across him like this the night before.

Suddenly consumed with worry once again, he decided to detour to Bobby's cabin on his way home and look in on the poor guy, just to be sure he wasn't suffering from anything more than a slight hangover.

"Hey! Bobby!" He shouted, banging on the door. "You home?"

No answer. Convinced he would have seen him throughout the day if Bobby had bothered to leave home, he entered without invitation, figuring Bobby might be resting, but it was worth disturbing him if it meant his mind would be at ease.

"You awake?"

The cabin was quiet, but it was also a damn mess. The cot Bobby slept on had been turned over and ashes spilled out of the open door of the woodstove.

"Bobby? What's going on here?"

A tiny whimper came from a corner behind a wooden chair and Frederick followed the noise to find Bobby wrapped in a blanket, huddled against the wall and shaking like a mouse about to be squished by a snake.

Bobby's eyes snapped up to meet his. "What are you doing here?" he barked at Frederick.

"You missed work today. The bosses won't be pleased when they hear about it."

"Good news for you, isn't it?"

"Huh?"

"Plenty more work for you if I'm not around."

Frederick noticed an empty whiskey bottle on the floor.

"Come on, Bobby. It's been a hard couple days but you got to get up now." He reached for his friend's arm, unprepared for a sudden burst of strength to come over Bobby as he shoved Frederick away from him as hard as he could. Frederick landed with a thud among the mess of cookware on the floor.

"Get out!" Bobby shouted at him. "I see you watching us every day, the quiet one, the one nobody would ever suspect, right? Planning your move, letting us come to trust you so you can take us for all we got."

"What are you babbling about?"

"I was born here! This land doesn't belong to you but here you are, taking our jobs, taking our money, all you lazy bastards flocking here to where you don't belong, thinking you can strike it rich just 'cause you can swing an axe and taking men like me for a fool. I don't want your help. Nobody wants your help."

He wrapped the blanket tightly around himself again and shrank back into his corner. In a split second he'd gone from shouting awful things to uncontrollably sobbing like a baby.

Frederick wondered what to do. He didn't want to leave his friend in such a pitiful state, but there didn't seem to be much point in staying here just to be screamed at. If Frederick had to manage a child's tantrum, he'd be much happier to go home and be with Moses.

So Frederick dusted off his hat and walked out the front door to do just that.

* * *

The next day was worse.

The rain came down even harder and even though Brisbee had attached the block to the top of the spar the day before, one good yank on the rope caused it to come tumbling down and crash into the ground so hard it made a crater at their feet.

Another close call.

A younger man named Pete seemed to be even more nervous than Frederick; he stood off to the side of the ruckus and tried not to hyperventilate. Another man, Ace, wasn't so calm. He confronted Brisbee and started screaming at him, taking off his hat and throwing it to the ground.

"Hey, hey, hey... take it down a notch, will you Ace?" Frederick interjected. "It's wet and slippery. Brisbee didn't mean to do anything wrong. Take a breath." He noticed Pete nearby, shaking from nerves. "Better yet, take a walk, both of you. Get your head right, then we can try this again."

"Don't you go thinkin' *you* can tell me what to do," Ace snarled at him, and Frederick got the message of what he really meant. No matter how cooperative these white men were with Frederick on the surface, it was always there, that ugly sense of superiority on their part that gave Frederick every reason to think any one of them would turn their backs on him in a second when the chips were down.

Still, Ace knew the suggestion was a good one and put his soaking wet hat back on his head for some stubborn reason, then ventured off into the woods with Pete on his heels.

The rest of the day was a bust. Four men short, since Bobby still hadn't come back either, and defeated by the relentless rain, the men hadn't succeeded in their task and the tree looked just as it had the day before.

Hours later, when Ace and Pete still hadn't come back from the woods, Frederick decided it was time to have a talk with the boss.

* * *

"Come in," the boss logger instructed. His office was small, but warm. He wore a nice wool suit that Frederick envied standing here in his work boots, soaked to the bone. "What may I do for you..."

"Frederick."

"Frederick. Frederick what?"

"Just Frederick is fine."

"Just Frederick it is. So, Frederick, what brings you to my office?"

"I'm worried about the crew, sir."

"Is this about the accident earlier this week?"

"No, sir, not exactly. I believe something dangerous is out in the woods."

The boss logger laughed. "Of course there are dangerous things out in the woods, everybody knows that."

"Something else sir, not just a wild animal. The other night I saw something rip apart a bear like it was a no more than a rag doll. Yesterday a man... well, he changed somehow, I don't know why exactly, and today two men went for a walk in the woods and never came back."

"What did you see? The thing that ate the bear, what was it?"

"It was dark, sir. I'm sure I don't know what in the hell it was. I just know it was big."

"A bigger bear, then?"

"I've never known a bear to ruthlessly attack one of its own. Few animals will do that. Except for men, of course."

The boss logger shrugged. "There are plenty of wolves, mountain lions, all kinds of predators in those woods. My suggestion is that you and the rest of the men avoid venturing out there alone, especially in the dark as you have, and keep focusing on your work."

"About the work, sir, today wasn't especially fruitful. Between the rain and being short handed—"

"What do you mean short handed? Why?"

"Like I said, we have a man dead, a man... indisposed, and two more missing."

"That's only four men. The rest of you should be able to handle it. And if you can't, perhaps this just isn't the profession for you."

Frederick squeezed the brim of his soaking wet hat. Water dripped into a puddle on the wood floor of the office.

"Tell each of them to pull it together and get the job done tomorrow. I'll be by to check your work. And in the mean time, stay out of the woods."

Frederick had nothing left to add, and he'd had enough conversations like this one to know when something was a dead end. Declining to argue any further, he nodded and left to head home for the day.

*   *   *

His mind was preoccupied with worry all through supper. Not even the smell of freshly baked bread and salmon on the plate in front of him made him feel any more at ease. He hadn't planned to tell Aponi, but she knew him too well and pried it out of him. So, he told her everything, realizing mid-sentence that all of it, but especially the encounter with Bobby, had shaken him up more than he had known.

She looked him straight in the eye when he spoke, as she always did, and listened to every word before reacting to any of them. A sign of love if there ever was one. "There are plenty of stories about beasts in the woods around here," she said once he had finished his tale. "We all heard them as children."

She noticed the tension in his body and placed a reassuring hand on his arm.

"They were just legends. Our parents would warn us about greed or anger corrupting our soul and tell us we'd become monsters with a taste for human flesh, expelled from our tribe, doomed to wander alone in the cold woods forever."

"So the monsters were men once?"

She shrugged. "They're stories meant to teach us that the woods have their secrets. They can love you, they can protect you, or they can kill you."

"How do you know which?"

"What's found in nature is found in men. All things beautiful and all things bad. If you do your best to do right by the land and by your people, the woods will do right by you."

Frederick considered this. "So something might look for the bad in a person. But can something in the woods change a person? It didn't eat Bobby. It just made him... different."

"Maybe. Or maybe nothing made him different and it's just the grieving. Pain changes people all the time."

"Yeah. Yeah, I guess it does."

She moved closer and leaned her head up against his.

"If you think something bad is out there, something probably is. Go back and see Bobby again. See what he knows. You can't handle it if you don't know what it is you're dealing with."

The orange glow from the woodstove shone on the side of her face and brought out the many shades of brown in her round eyes. She could be a few miles east with her people, and he knew she missed them dearly, but here she was in this little cabin with him. Those brown eyes were his whole entire world.

* * *

From the moment Frederick approached Bobby's cabin, he could feel in his bones that it was colder inside it than it was out in the rain. The door was ajar, probably still open from when Frederick had run out the day before.

"Bobby, I'm coming in," he announced. "We need to talk."

The inside looked exactly the same. A disaster. Dark. Freezing cold. It didn't look as if Bobby had bothered to light a fire in the wood stove overnight.

It was so quiet, Frederick thought for a moment that the cabin was empty. Until he heard a grunting sound and his blood ran cold. The animal was here.

A heavy footstep, then another. He backed away slowly but did not make it out the door before it emerged from the shadows.

It was hideous. The kind of creature that only forms in a man's darkest nightmares. It walked on two legs like a man, it had two long arms like a man, but it was abnormally tall. Its massive frame hunched under the ceiling, its backbone was razor sharp and protruded from its skin, and its eyes were a shade of black so deep Frederick wondered if it had eyes at all, or if it just had two holes in its horrible face, windows to the dark nothingness of the creature's very soul. And at the top of its head was a cluster of antlers, all tangled together like a hellish crown of thorns. Blood dripped onto its snout from its forehead where the horns met its skin. Its entire body was a pale blue, so pale it was almost white, as if it were made of ice.

Worst of all, it held a bleeding red mass in its hand. A muscle. A heart.

Blood dripped down its chin and Frederick realized it had been feeding on something. And unless the creature had thought to drag the remnants of the slaughtered bear or some other prey into the cabin, that something must have been Bobby.

The creature looked straight down at Frederick in a terrifying standoff before it inhaled a huge breath and shrieked louder than any noise Frederick had ever heard.

And Frederick ran faster than he ever thought he could run.

*   *   *

"It came back for Bobby," he said as he burst into the cabin. "It came back and ate him. Grab your coat and your warmest boots. We need to run."

"Slow down..."

"No time. Let's go. Now."

He picked up Moses, who fussed and squirmed in his arms, confused and scared. Aponi reached for the child and Frederick handed him over, deciding instead to rifle through the cabinets and take any food he could find.

"Where?"

"Anywhere. To be with your family, I guess. No. What if it follows us? We need to be alone."

"We can't just run away."

"We damn well can and we damn well will."

"My people are here. Your people are here."

"These men are not my people. They'll need to look after themselves."

Aponi stomped her foot to the floor. "Stop!" She cried. Moses burrowed his face into his mother's shoulder.

"We don't know what we're running to. Out there alone it could be worse. What if there are more? And we'll have other monsters, too. Bears, mountain lions. No shelter, no food. I won't take my child into the woods to freeze to death in the rain."

Stuck between a rock and a hard place was where he suddenly found himself. He knew she was right, but if his life as a nomad across the continent had taught him anything, it was that if you're too close to danger, it was best not to linger until the danger found you and it'd be too late.

"I can't protect us from this. It's too big."

"You don't have to do it yourself. You can't do it yourself. Tell the others. Whether you think of them as your people or not doesn't matter now. We're safer together and you know that's true."

And he did know it. But somehow, it scared him more than the thought of facing this thing alone.

* * *

Mustering up the gumption to explain all this to a crew of men, most of whom Frederick hadn't even spoken to once before, was an uncomfortable feat, to say the least.

The crew did not expect the quietest man of them all to come running over the hill screaming for help, that was for sure. They watched him tear down to the site, sliding in the mud and shouting at the top of his lungs and surely did not know what to make of it. Standing at the ready to pull down a beast of a spruce tree, a few of them even felt annoyed that Frederick was late.

They were going to laugh him right off of the job site, Frederick was convinced of it. And then what? He'd be left alone to battle this monster, whatever it was, and would most likely lose. Hell, even if he had just gone crazy and imagined the whole thing, he was probably out of a job.

Catching his breath, Frederick did his best to relay the confusing tale.

It took an eternity for someone to finally pipe up.

"I just knew something awful happened to Pete and Ace," said Brisbee. "It ain't like them to up and leave their post like that."

A young man named Burke nodded, even though, at the tender age of eighteen, he hadn't been here long enough to know what was usual for Pete and Ace or what wasn't. But he still had that youthful hunger to work hard and prove himself, so vanishing from a job was something that wouldn't make sense to him at all.

Another long moment passed without a word, just the noise of rain pummeling the already enormous puddles around their feet.

"So what, then?" Frederick asked, impatient. "You believe me, or don't you?"

The men looked at each other. One of them shrugged.

"Well," said a man whose name Frederick did not know, "I sure haven't seen nothing like that before, but these woods are dangerous. So whatever it is, a monster like you say, or some wild creature that wandered here from some cave, it's causing a problem. It almost don't matter what exactly it is."

The man looked back to the huge spar tree, fully loaded with the heavy block and the web of ropes intended to move some of nature's most powerful creations.

"I reckon we could use this to try and take it down."

The others nodded in agreement.

"Sure," another said. "That spruce won't be going nowhere. We can get back to it tomorrow."

They all looked to Frederick as if to wait for his approval of the plan. He nodded, surprised by how easy the conversation had turned out to be. "OK. We can do that," was all he managed to say.

* * *

The moon was a tiny sliver in the sky, hardly casting any light onto Frederick as he sat alone on a cold, wet tree stump.

Frederick knew the men were all putting their reputations on the line with the boss logger for putting off the spruce for a whole other day, and he also knew none of them had seen yet what they would be dealing with. For those reasons, Frederick was the one to sit outside in the freezing cold and act as bait.

He didn't know a whole hell of a lot about this thing, but since it first found a bear grieving for her cub and then came for the broken shell of the man who used to be Bobby, Frederick figured it looked for pain. If pain was what it wanted, pain was something he had to offer.

The rain stopped and the forest was quiet, save for the sounds of owls on the hunt for critters that scurried around in the brush, and it was in that quiet, a space Frederick had so frequently found a sense of safety, that he now went all the way to the deepest, darkest corners of his mind, the corners he hoped never to show to Moses. The night a group of men rode by his childhood bedroom carrying torches and threw bricks into the window, laughing, drunk, and finding the terror of a young child to be the funniest thing they'd ever seen. The ghastly imaginations of the war. The fear that lived an inch beneath his skin at every moment, that pushed him to move farther and farther away from the horrible things that happened to men who looked just like he did.

And worst of all was the fear that something would happen to his child. That happy, innocent, chubby little thing that knew nothing of life aside from playtime in the mud puddles outside and falling asleep to the sound of his mother's lullabies.

It felt like hours that he sat there. Alone. Wondering if the men would bother having his back or if they would just leave him there to become the creature's next meal.

Frederick's breath hung in the air. His eyes felt heavy and wide open at the same time.

Then, a growling sound.

He stayed perfectly still and waited. And waited. And waited for it to creep just a little closer to him.

It emerged from the woods, snarling, groaning, hunched over with the weight of that enormous tangle of horns on its misshapen head. Its black eyes focused on Frederick, who had to fight every single nerve in his body not to run as far and as fast as he could from this hideous thing.

It stopped and stared. It took a deep breath and shrieked like a banshee, its shrill cry carrying over the cliffs and straight out to the ocean.

"Go!" A voice shouted from the woods.

The men all snapped into action, emerging from their shadowy hiding places and scattering to their posts.

Brisbee ran to the base of the spar tree and set out a bunch of ropes. Burke ran in a big circle and set out several lanterns so that most of the men, six of them, at least, could run to the big log they had rigged up in preparation for this.

"Haul!"

The men pulled on a long rope as hard as they could to raise the log high in the air.

But it was heavy.

The first man at the head of the line lost his footing and couldn't stand up straight in the mud anymore. He fell to his side and let go of the rope, causing two more men to trip over him and almost drop the log before it was ready.

They were scared. The creature knew it.

It turned to see them sliding around in the muck and took a heavy step forward, and Frederick was struck with the thought that he didn't know a handful of these men, and in a matter of moments, he may never get the chance.

"Pull!" Shouted Brisbee, who ran away from his post near the spar tree and scrambled to help them.

The monster breathed deep and grunted at the men, but then, as if it had heard Frederick's own thoughts calling it to let them be, it slowly turned its attention back to him.

Frederick stood up and looked into its eyes, as dark as ever, even in the soft glow of the lanterns that surrounded them. It was tall. Taller than it had seemed when it was freshly fed and hunched over in Bobby's cabin. It looked at him. It studied him. Frederick felt that time had stopped. Nothing in the world existed but the terror he felt in this moment.

It opened its mouth wide, bearing its repulsive, tangled teeth, when the log came swinging like a pendulum, crashing into the creature and knocking it over to its side.

"Drop it!" Brisbee yelled, and everyone let go of the rope, causing the log to plummet downward. It landed on top of the fallen beast and pinned it to the ground.

It struggled and screamed and thrashed its head from side to side. Brisbee ran fast back to his assortment of ropes at the base of the spar tree, tied a lasso and threw it to Frederick, who then threw it toward the monster's neck. His hands shook and he missed; the rope landed in the mess of horns, causing a violent tug-of-war between the two of them as the beast thrashed under the weight crushing its pale body.

Frederick managed to pull the rope back and try again with a bigger loop, then again, then again until it finally landed in a circle big enough for its entire head and Frederick could pull the rope tight around its throat.

So heavy and so powerful the creature was, Frederick hardly kept himself standing upright, sliding around in the mud and not daring to let the rope slip out of his hands.

The monster's ugly shriek became a tiny, high pitched yelping noise. Frederick pulled tighter and tighter until its body stopped moving and its eyes gazed gently up to his.

Suddenly, it was still. But the creature wasn't dead, not yet - he could tell by its breath in the cold night air.

It wanted to speak with him.

Careful not to let go of the rope, Frederick inched closer.

"Stay back!" Brisbee cried. "It's almost dead! Yank hard and snap its neck!"

Frederick just stared at the monster in the dim lantern light.

"What the hell are you waiting for?" Brisbee yelled, but Frederick gave no response.

When he approached its face, a whisper came to him, even though the monster's mouth didn't move.

"It hurts," it said to him in a venomous hiss. *"It hurts me. I am dying. I can feel myself rot."*

"What are you?" Frederick asked without having to speak.

"I am the earth. I am the place where your darkest thoughts go when you sleep at night. I am darkness itself."

"Why do you harm us?"

"Your pain eases my pain. I see pain in you and I want to drink it from inside your heart."

It lunged for him but barely moved under the crushing weight of the log, causing it to squirm in frustration.

"Your heart," it hissed at Frederick. *"Give me your heart."*

"You cannot have it," Frederick replied. *"My heart is not mine to give. My heart belongs to those for whom I would do anything. Even die. I will not die for you."*

It groaned and closed its eyes.

Frederick stared down at the monster, its face covered in mud and its black eyes slowly blinking at him. *"You say you feel yourself rot. When the rot begins, death has happened already. You stay alive by feeding on pain. I could keep you alive, but instead, I will let you rot."*

Frederick reached deep into every muscle of his body and yanked on the lasso with a force he had never known. The entire crew heard the bone snap. The monster went limp. Before their eyes, its body began to decay, melting into the mud and leaving behind a broken skeleton underneath the heavy log.

The rest of the crew crept up to it with a cautious curiosity. After a long moment of silence, Brisbee gently placed a hand on Frederick's shoulder.

"Go home," he said to him. "The rest of us will get set up for tomorrow. You did good tonight."

*　　*　　*

The bodies of Pete and Ace were found torn apart the next day, but thankfully, they were the last. The monster had been hungry. If Frederick hadn't seen to it that the monster was taken down, there's no telling where the killing would have ended.

The life of a logger was hard enough, and on some nights when Frederick couldn't sleep, he wondered if more of them would come looking for the pain that lingered beneath the surface of so many men, especially his own.

But months passed, then a year, then two. Life in the camp town wasn't perfect, and some days it wasn't even good, but it was all right. And if that were to ever change, Frederick had worked hard enough in his life to know that he could take care of his family just about anywhere if they needed to leave again.

Moses was in school now and spent his days learning to read and write. Days off the job site were spent visiting Aponi's tribe or teaching Moses about the forest they called home. Those were the best days, when it was just the three of them outside, when the boy's wonder slowly turned into familiarity and a confidence began to build once he knew how to handle himself out here.

It wasn't an easy life, and it never would be. For now though, the woods were still, their son was happy, and their home was safe.

The Miner

Baker's Park, CO

1868

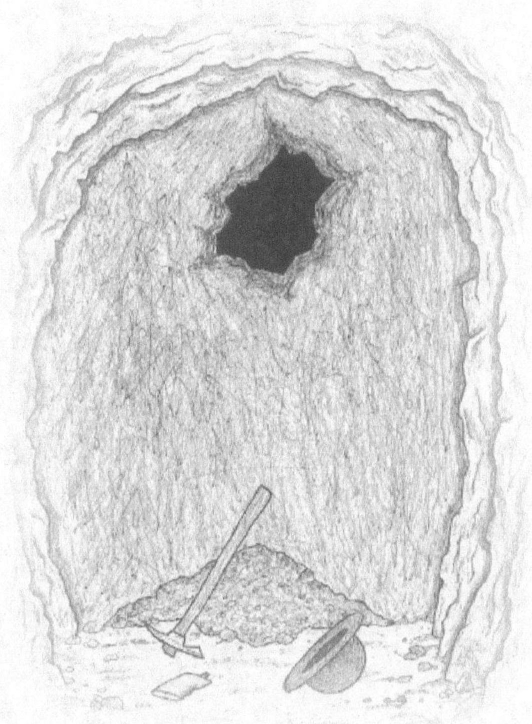

By the time the whistle blew, Al had nearly forgotten he was working. He had been trapped in his own thoughts for hours, mindlessly swinging the pickaxe into the hard rocks inside the Colorado mountains. It was fall, and the skies would already be dark once he ascended to the surface in that sweaty, disgusting metal lift with all the other sweaty, disgusting men. They would stumble to the saloon and drink their body weight in beer, like they did every night, and Al would feel refreshed for a minute or two before the aches set in all over his body.

He scoffed at the place even daring to call itself a saloon - it wasn't like there were any girls to look at. Its one and only purpose was this damn mine, the dark hole in the earth where men like him would sweat and toil their lives away in hopes that the bosses would give them a slim piece of the riches they found inside it.

The beer was salty tonight, and the so-called saloon was dead save for Al and the rest of the crew. The younger guys palled around and made crude jokes until it was time to go home to their wives - if they were lucky enough to have found a wife. The older ones, like Al, kept to themselves and drank until they got bored enough to stumble home in the cold autumn air, pass out on a cot, and do it all again tomorrow.

He walked by a group of ladies on the corner wearing their fanciest dresses. Of course, that wasn't saying much. They were mostly widows, all old enough that their kids had grown up and moved away, leaving their mothers to turn tricks or starve. One of them had to be in her seventies by now.

Al had succumbed to the temptation once or twice in his younger days, but now he just saw their company as a waste of his hard-earned money. Some nights he'd give them a polite nod on his way home, but tonight he kept his head down and walked right by.

"Evening, Al."

Mabel was trying to get his attention. He'd taken a shine to her a while back. She had followed the rush just like the rest of them and made a pretty penny on the excited young miners, but a tragic accident had crushed one of her hips and it had never healed quite right, so leaving to go somewhere else was out of the question. She was stuck here and trying to make any kind of living she could, just like he was.

Al had never married or had a family. What was the point?

Damn little brats just grew up and left you hanging, just like those poor widows.

He had flocked to Colorado years ago with hundreds of men from all over the range looking for riches, but found that the only assholes getting rich in this operation were the bosses at the top. They lived up on the hill in their nice houses, paid for proper schooling for their kids, and left the rest of the town to wither away as they struggled to get deeper and deeper into the mountains, searching for deposits in the hills that had long since run empty.

Al had managed to save a penny or two with no mouths to feed, but it was never enough to go on a search for a proper life. And now, pushing fifty and with damn near nothing to offer, Al had learned how to keep to his business and live alone in the quiet.

His cabin was small and had nearly nothing inside it. A cot, a wood stove, a few dirty pots and pans, and an empty, rusted flask he never got around to refilling. The whiskey in this town was terrible.

Here he was in this dump, remembering how he'd thought he had nothing as a kid. He scoffed at his younger, more arrogant self. Pa had built them a home. It wasn't much, just a house out in the middle of nowhere on the plains, where the cold wind slapped him across the face and stung him in the eyes, but it was a home, all right. It had bedrooms, a proper fireplace, a dining table and everything. And Pa had done that as nothing but a simple rancher. Al and his three younger sisters may have been bored out of their minds, but there was always wood for the fire and food on the table.

He used to wonder what life would have been like had Ma lived longer. Al must have been about eight years old when the youngest killed her. Every month Ma's belly got a little bigger and her face got a little paler. The smell of meat made her sick, and she grew too tired to tend to the kids. Then when that little monster finally decided to come out, she brought all of Ma's blood with her.

The blood. Al had never seen so much blood, not before or since. And here was this little alien creature who'd killed their mother and now demanded all the attention in the house. As the oldest, it fell to him to look after the little ones - all three of them - and keep helping Pa on the property every day, too. This went on for years until the oldest girl, Maddie, finally got big enough to handle the house and the younger kids.

Maybe that was why he'd never tried too hard to find a wife.

Children were loud and obnoxious; they spilled the milk from the cows and dropped all the eggs before they even got them out of the coop. They screamed all night and followed him around all day asking stupid questions.

"How does the corn come out of the ground?"

"Why don't the chickens fly away when we're not looking?"

"Why do I have to take a bath?"

And worst of all, *"When is Mama coming back?"*

He wasn't cut out for it, plain and simple. When mines started opening all over the West, he jumped on the opportunity to finally leave home and make a fortune - it would be far more than Pa ever had as a rancher, that was for damn sure.

But he hadn't planned on the war cutting into his prospects. He'd been mining for a few years already when the fighting broke out and lots of younger men went off to battle, leaving older men like Al to shoulder the burden of the extra work. He worked all day, every day, barely pausing to eat, until his back finally gave out. He was out of work for months and spent too much of his hard earned money on that awful whiskey, the only thing that dulled the pain, and the company of the ladies on the corner, the only thing that dulled the aching sense of sadness.

Then, just as he was ready to get back to it, mining camps all over the territory found themselves in a bit of a pickle: they'd dug up just about all the gold they could, and less and less of it was coming out every day, which meant less and less of the profits went into Al's pocket.

All the while, years worth of stories from the Gold Rush all the way out in California swirled around his head. It was still going strong out there - it had to be, given the sheer size of the properties. It would take years - decades, even - to clear all the gold out of those hills.

California... now that was an idea. He was getting fed up with the Colorado winters. The cold had started to create a different kind of pain deep in his bones. He felt it every time the wind howled and every time another icicle formed outside his window. He was done with the ice and snow, and now every time the cold wind blew, he thought of sunshine and gold.

He had some money saved up, but at this rate it'd take many more years to be enough. The trek would take weeks. He'd be going through rocky mountain passes - deadly in the winter - and long stretches of desert - deadly in the summer. He'd need to do it right, with a proper horse and wagon and plenty of food, water, and blankets. It'd be a tough journey, but once he made it there, it'd be worth it. He pictured huge valleys bathed in yellow sunshine, flowers blooming in all directions, and even the sparkling ocean. California was paradise, and once he'd made his fortune in gold, he could retire by the sea.

Unless, of course, he died here in this sad little cabin before he could even start the journey.

* * *

Al stood in a narrow tunnel, with the dim glow of the gas lamps behind him barely lighting the way, and swung the pickaxe into the wall. He thought of those rich assholes on the hill, counting their cut of the gold he himself was digging out of the rocks in the sweltering heat or the freezing cold.

He swung the axe harder, thinking of those men who'd made it to California, panning for gold in sparkling rivers in the sunshine. He clenched his jaw and thought of those younger men who'd marched off to a war that meant nothing to them - it wasn't like the western territories had any intention of breaking from the Union, no matter what happened in the South. He grunted as he swung the axe into the rock, harder and harder, his face turning red and his hands chaffing against the wooden handle.

Finally, he beat the wall as hard as he could and startled himself when the axe broke through.

He kept at it, pieces of rock cascading down to the ground, dirt flying everywhere, hurting his eyes and making him cough. He kept going until there was a hole large enough to see through, then lifted a small lantern and peered behind the rock wall.

There was some kind of empty space, all right. It looked like a hollow section of a dead tree, where small woodland animals would hide nuts and twigs for the upcoming winter. He squinted in the soft light, and as his eyes slowly adjusted, he could swear he saw something glisten.

He set the lantern down and kept at it with the axe, making the hole just wide enough for his head and shoulders. He peered in again, this time leaning into the opening for a better view.

The space was hardly bigger than he was, but it was packed with treasure. Huge chunks of lead sat there, glistening with streaks of silver, as if they'd been waiting for him. He rubbed his eyes, convinced the soft light of the lantern was playing tricks on him. But the more he stared, the more they sparkled.

The whistle blew, jolting Al out of his stupor so hard he banged the back of his head on the rock before squeezing back out of the hole. He looked at his fellow men, all wiping sweat from their foreheads and yanking off gloves, letting their skin breathe as much as it could under the rough calluses. None seemed to notice Al or the nook where he was standing.

He dimmed the light and let the other men exit to the shaft before him, careful not to call any attention to his discovery. It would take hours and lots of extra hands to break down more of the wall and haul the pieces of lead out of the mine, so there was no point in alerting any of them now that they were all heading to the bar or home for the night.

Still, it felt wrong to leave it there, partially exposed. He felt like it needed protection, which Al knew to be a ridiculous notion. Who would it need protecting from all the way down here in the deep recesses of the earth? The bats? That was just crazy. No, he could set the axe down for the night and come back to it tomorrow. For now, he needed a drink.

* * *

The usual crew congregated at the saloon: the old timers like Al and any young man who wasn't in the doghouse with his wife - or worse, newly married and still in love with her. Al drank his beer and allowed himself to enjoy the cold liquid running down his dry throat.

It was already dark outside, and Al felt a chill run through his body. Could he take it for another winter? Every night he emerged from the mine covered in sweat, which meant his wet clothes nearly froze as soon as he stepped out into the frigid mountain air.

Al ordered another beer, then another. The rest of the men headed home for the night, but Al continued to sit there, sipping and staring out the window, first at the fancy homes on the hill, then at the mine. That damned mine. That dark, dank hole in the ground. It wasn't an opening into the mountain so much as it was a gateway to Hell. The heat, the darkness, the aches all over his body made him feel like that old myth of Sisyphus pushing that boulder up a hill, over and over again for all eternity. Such had become Al's fate, swinging that pickaxe for years and years and years, only to find more work to be done.

He stumbled out of the bar after he'd found himself the only man still on the premises and facing down an ugly stare from the barkeep, obviously ready to go home for the night. Al was less than eager to do so. Despite the long day's work and the drinks inside him, Al didn't feel the least bit tired.

And there it was, the opening of the mine. It usually repelled him, but now it seemed to call out to him, asking him to come back. Going home to his cabin would just result in Al staring at the ceiling until sleep finally came for him, but the mine offered him something he hadn't felt in over a decade: hope.

His future was in that mine, tucked away in the hollow nook full of riches. He could go back for it and none of the crew would be the wiser. He could hide the silver in his cabin until he procured a horse and wagon and get on the trail before the winter set in. He'd be long gone before any of the bosses on the hill even noticed.

He approached the mineshaft alone and in near total darkness. A lantern hung on the door to the lift, as if it had been placed there just for him.

As he reached for it, something fell out of his pocket and landed on the ground with a soft thud. He thought better of turning on the lantern; even though most of the town was home and in bed, there was always a chance someone could notice the light shimmering in the distance. He patted around in the dirt until he retrieved the fallen object: his tin flask. Al didn't remember bringing it with him today. He opened it and was instantly hit with the strong smell of whiskey, which struck him as odd since he certainly didn't remember refilling it at the bar, either.

But it didn't matter. He tucked the flask back in his pocket and stepped onto the lift, directing it to lower him into the shaft with the loud, metallic grinding sound of the gears.

It landed at the bottom with a heavy jolt and Al finally lit the lantern. The light was weak. It hadn't occurred to him just how little a single lantern could do in the total darkness of the mineshaft. There were usually dozens of them around while the men worked.

Soft squeaking sounds echoed through the chambers. The bats were all awake now and going about their business in the absence of the daytime light and noise. Al squinted and fumbled around to find a wheelbarrow, then made his way back to the nook.

There it was, the hole in the wall and the pickaxe just sitting there, waiting to be used. For some reason, he felt the need to lean in again to check and make sure the treasure was still there. An absurd thought, since no one else knew of it and the bats were hardly a cause of concern, but he checked nonetheless. There it sat, barely glistening in the dim light of the lantern.

He swung the axe as hard as he could, creating a larger opening in the wall, barely large enough for him to squeeze through. It would be tough to lift these huge chunks of lead into the wheelbarrow, but he was going to have to try. He kneeled down and traced the streaks of silver with his fingers. They were beautiful. Like tiny little rivers in the ugly grey block of lead.

They would be heavy.

A troubling thought occurred to him for the very first time: how in God's name did he even expect to get the silver out of the lead in the first place? All he'd ever done was dig chunks of gold out of the wall and toss them in the bin, where they'd eventually be sent to a whole other job site to be broken down and pressed into bars. Al had never done that before. How was he supposed to buy a horse and a wagon with a giant block of lead?

His heart sank at the realization. This was stupid. He shouldn't have come here for such a pointless mission. What the hell was he thinking, coming down here alone? He'd be lucky to get out without being bitten by a bat, or worse, trip over something in the dark and break a bone with no help anywhere nearby.

He sat next to the treasure and rubbed his temples, cursing himself for his own idiocy. He needed a drink. Luckily, there happened to be a flask full of whiskey in his pocket.

The whiskey tasted good. Much better than Al had remembered. It was so good he almost forgot why he had bothered to stop drinking it in the first place.

He looked at the silver rivers in the lead blocks and chuckled. He had no idea how he was going to properly extricate it, but he was going to try. He could bring them all back to his cabin and chip away at it, little by little, even if it took him months to figure it out.

He could request to move to the pressing facility and sneak in his own supply to press into silver bars, or even better, he could move onto the next mining town to do so, where no one would suspect he'd taken it from a different mine.

It might take a while to sort out, but Al had been doing this for years now, and it was worth a few more months to do it right.

He put the flask away and swung the axe at the wall. It didn't take long; ten or twelve swings of the pickaxe sent huge chunks of lead cascading into a pile at his feet as if he'd broken a dam.

Gathering up all his strength, he lifted the first block with every muscle in his body, then quickly turned back to the hole in the wall to chuck it into the wheelbarrow.

But as Al spun around, he nearly jumped backward when he saw it: the wall was perfectly intact. The hole he had created was gone.

He dropped the block of lead, missing his foot by barely an inch.

Every wall of the hollow nook was rock solid. But it couldn't be - he had just dug his way in here. Had parts of the ceiling collapsed and covered the hole while he wasn't looking? That must have been it. It was the only possible explanation. The good news was that the rocks would be easy to push through again if they had just loosened and fallen into place.

He swung hard with the pickaxe, expecting a pile of rocks to tumble to the ground with the slightest provocation, but it barely scraped the completely solid wall.

Al took another drink from the flask and resolved to get to work. He beat down the wall with all the force he could muster, just as he had the first time. It took about half an hour, or roughly that, as it was impossible to accurately track time down here in the darkness, but he made it through. He stepped through the opening in search of the wheelbarrow.

The wheelbarrow was nowhere to be found.

He lifted the lantern to further inspect the tunnel in the mine that had led to this mysterious spot.

Only it wasn't a tunnel at all. It was another small, hollow space, just like the one from which he had just emerged.

He must have broken down the wrong wall. That had to be it - he hadn't really inspected all four walls surrounding him before he had started with the axe. The wall he had come through in the first place had to be nothing but loose rocks from the ceiling. This was just the wrong one. He just needed to go back to the treasure and try again.

But as Al turned around to go back, the wall behind him was solid again. What the hell was going on? The darkness had to be playing tricks on him. One of these walls had an opening to where he had just been. It was just too damn dark to know for sure. To make matters worse, the lamplight was growing dim. It hadn't occurred to Al to check the level of lamp oil before coming down here. That was a stupid mistake. Shit.

He rubbed his eyes and took another shot of whiskey, then pressed his hands up against the rock wall. Solid. He moved around to each wall that surrounded him. Solid. Solid. Solid.

There was nothing to do but dig his way out again, though this time it would be harder; the space he found himself in now was even smaller than the nook that contained the treasure. There was barely enough range behind him to properly swing the axe for the desired impact on the wall. Still, he made do, swinging the axe over and over again until he could break through.

He squeezed through the new opening and gasped when the dull light shone onto the ground, revealing a skeleton slumped against a wall. The man, whoever he was, had been a miner, that was for sure. He wore a linen shirt and suspenders with a miner's hat, just like Al's.

Upon closer inspection, Al saw a tiny tin flask in the skeleton's hand. It looked just like his own, with a ring of rust around the top and a dent in the side. It looked exactly like his own, in fact. Had he dropped the flask when he stumbled in here? No, there it was, still in his pocket. As long as he had the flask in his hand, he figured, he might as well take another drink.

His head began to throb. The silver was nowhere to be found, but Al felt confident that it had been tucked away enough to avoid discovery in the morning. For now, he needed rest. The silver and his plans for the move to California could wait. It had been a stupid idea to come down here alone in the middle of the night. Now he was lost and growing confused, hungry, and tired, and suddenly that lumpy cot next to the wood stove in his cabin didn't seem so terrible.

One more drink, then he would work his way back the way

he came, through each hole in the wall until he reached the lift. For once, he longed to feel the cold mountain air on his face as he ascended back to civilization.

But again, Al turned to find all four walls of the enclosure to be solidly intact.

Panic began to set in. This wasn't a matter of getting lost and there was no way debris from the ceiling could have fallen and closed every opening he had created. His mind returned to those infernal Sunday school classes Pa had made him sit through as a child and their vivid descriptions of Hell, the fiery pit below the surface of the earth that hungered for the tortured souls of badly behaved boys and girls. He thought of Sisyphus and that damned boulder. He thought of Mabel and some of the other whores he had paid to keep him company while he was injured and suddenly believed in the concept of sin for the first time in his life. Had he died in the mine that day? Was he being punished?

Nonsense. Al was very much alive and the throbbing pain in his head proved it. But he wouldn't be for much longer if he didn't find his way out. He'd end up like this poor bastard on the ground. If there was a way into this mess, there was sure to be a way out of it, too.

Al pressed his ear up against a rock wall. If these walls were sealing up behind him, however that could be the case, the rock couldn't be that thick. And so far he had found more and more openings to crawl into, which meant he was finding enough hollow space below the mountain to create a whole new tunnel. All he had to do was connect these little rooms to one another. That was it, just a puzzle to be solved.

He stepped back and started breaking it down, yet again. He felt a sense of elation, mixed with a curious feeling of déjà vu, when the axe broke through. The rock crumbled easier this time; in fact, Al nearly lost control of the axe and let it fly through the hole in the wall. He kept at it until he could fit through the opening and peer inside.

But this time, there was nothing to see. He leaned through the hole as far as he could, lantern out in front of him, and saw nothing but darkness.

That couldn't be. He was on solid ground; it couldn't just disappear on the other side of a wall. He wriggled backwards, picked up the largest rock he could find, and chucked it through the opening, waiting for a thump on the dirt below. It never came.

He found another and dropped it on the ground, barely missing his own foot and the leg of the skeleton nearby.

THUD. It wasn't his hearing that was the problem.

On the other side of this wall was a black hole, an empty space to nowhere. A draft crept in and slithered around his bare neck and his sweat-drenched shirt. His blood suddenly ran cold.

He drank more whiskey just to feel the warmth land in his gut. Somehow the flask hadn't run out just yet. He couldn't tell if the bitter liquid was helping his pounding headache or making it worse.

The black hole just sat there, staring at him. He couldn't explain it, and the thought of an emptiness so vast and cold laying in the middle of the earth scared the daylights out of him. He knew that wherever that opening might take him, he needed to go in the opposite direction.

Al picked up the axe and swung it again. His hands were so raw and chapped they began to bleed. Suddenly the axe felt heavier than the biggest bull Al had ever handled back on the ranch. It felt heavier than those huge blocks of lead he had waiting for him back in the first chamber. It felt as though all those years of hard labor had crashed onto his shoulders all at once.

He kept swinging, his arms aching so bad tears began to flow from his eyes, stinging like hell as dust and dirt flew into them. As soon as the opening was large enough, he threw the axe in ahead of him and began to push his way through.

Shit. The hole wasn't quite big enough after all. He found himself stuck at the shoulders and writhing as hard as he could. The jagged edges of the wall tore up his shirt and the skin underneath it; his arms bled as he slowly inched forward into the space ahead of him.

Finally, his shoulders were free, and the rest of his body tumbled to the ground after them. The wall had scraped his body and punched him in the gut. He was exhausted and in pain, but he was on solid ground. He had managed to escape the black hole, and tried to take solace in that fact.

His lungs heaved and the air inside them felt like daggers. The tears came again. All of it started to gush from his eyes: the exhaustion, the confusion, the pain, and the fear.

Part of him wanted to be disgusted with himself. He was a blubbering, drunken mess stuck in the mine that had trapped him for years. But most of him didn't have the strength to care anymore. Here he was, scraped and covered in every fluid his body could produce, a man lost in the depths of the earth. His sense of hope slipped away by the second.

It felt like hours before Al could open his swollen eyes. Maybe it was. It was pitch black all around him, and he realized the lantern was missing. The axe he had thrown into the hole ahead of him, but the lantern he had not. Now the hole, like the many before it, had closed, and the light was gone. He began to sob again, but it was weaker now, the cries not of panic, but a devastating defeat.

His arms fell to his side and he jumped when his hand landed in a pool of warm liquid. Water? It couldn't be. It was thicker than water. He lifted his hand up to his nose, but couldn't smell anything other than dirt mixed with his own sweat.

He gently licked at it, attempting to find a taste. It had a slight metallic sense to it. It was...blood? That didn't make any sense, unless it was his own. Was he bleeding so bad it was dripping and forming pools on the ground? If he was bleeding that bad, he'd need a doctor quick, or he wouldn't have much time left. But the alternative might have been even worse: if it wasn't his blood, it must have been someone else's.

His throat felt drier than dust, but he managed to croak out a single word.

"Hello?"

No answer. But there was a slight echo against the rocks, which made him shiver.

"Who's there?"

Still nothing. If this was someone else's blood, that someone was surely dead.

Warmth crept up along his legs. For a minute Al thought he had hit the point of exhaustion where he no longer had control of his bladder and had pissed himself. But no, the sensation was outside and slowly seeping into his pants, not the other way around. It was more of the metallic substance. It was more blood.

It seemed to be spreading, so much so that he couldn't even feel a dry patch of dirt on the ground.

It had to be coming from somewhere. There was either a body

in this room with him or it was leaking in through the walls. With no light, there was only one way to find out.

On his hands and knees, he crawled around the perimeter of the hollow chamber. Nothing so far but a firm wall pressed against his side and the pools of blood splashing underneath his hands.

He felt around on the walls, hoping to find cracks where a leak could be coming from. He imagined the bloody handprints he must have been leaving on the rock. Someone would find this tunnel one day and who knows what they would think: that some kind of ritual had taken place here, something depraved, something violent, or that this had been the sight of some other unspeakable crime.

As he searched, his breath became deeper, and soon, faint sobs began to fill the air. It took a few minutes for Al to realize the sobs didn't belong to him. They were shrill unrelenting, like a child crying for its mother's attention, and made the pounding in his head much, much worse. Where was it coming from? He covered his ears with both his hands and paced around the space, stepping in puddles and bumping into walls in the darkness.

"Stop!" He shouted to nothing in particular.

Al banged his fists against the walls and continued searching for any opening that could be the source of the blood or the noise. Finally, his arms stretched high above him, and he felt something: a tiny crack where the wall met the ceiling. He scratched at it with his bare hands and small pieces of rock tumbled down, mostly landing on his face and hair.

The axe. Where the hell was the axe? It didn't even matter any more. Al was so desperate he couldn't find a spare second to look around again in the dark. He kept digging and scratching until his fingernails began to fall off.

The crying grew louder.

"Stop! Stop it! Enough!"

But the cries continued.

He used all his strength to pull himself up and through the hole, tumbling through it and crashing onto his back on the other side.

For a brief moment, he felt his entire body go into shock, but seconds later, the pain shot all the way up his spine and into his neck. This was bad. He'd broken something on the fall and his entire body froze. He couldn't move his legs. He could hardly breathe.

But the cries had stopped. It was quiet.

Al managed to scoot himself to an upright position and lean back against the wall. He reached for the flask again, which somehow, though he couldn't possibly explain it, was still nearly half-full.

The whiskey burned his dry throat, but seemed to soothe it at the same time. His eyelids felt heavy. So heavy. Suddenly his eyes hurt more than any of the cuts, fractured bones, or aching muscles in the rest of his body.

He drank more and more until he finally reached the bottom of the flask. How had there been so much whiskey in that tiny thing? It didn't matter. Nothing mattered. It was dark and it was quiet. And Al needed to rest.

*   *   *

It wasn't unusual for men to abandon a mine without a moment's notice. It was hard work, and many miners did it until the day their bodies just couldn't take it anymore. Men would wander away in search of a simpler life on a farm or even head into the cities to seek an easier form of employment.

It was awfully lucky for Mabel that she had stumbled onto Al's empty cabin before anyone else. Every now and then, she would work her way through the miner's quarters, and nearly every night, someone would take her up on her offer, even if they'd declined her hours before. Al hadn't done so in several years now, so she usually didn't bother anymore. But something told her to drop by, and when Al wasn't home and hadn't made an appearance at the saloon all day, something also told her he wasn't coming back.

She was the one who found his money tucked behind the wood stove in a leather pouch. If Al came back, she figured she'd return it. But if not, it'd finally be time to hang up her garters for good.

It was a few years before the men down in the mineshaft were ready to lay tracks in a new tunnel. The gold had dried up, but the continued pressure to find something of value in the hills meant the camp had to expand into new territory.

It took days to properly break the rock down without threatening the foundation of the mine itself, but once they had done it and the hollow space opened before them, each and every man on the crew stood there in disbelief, rubbing their eyes and turning up the lamp light to be sure they weren't hallucinating.

Before them lay a skeleton, dressed in mining clothes just like theirs, with a tin flask at its side. How the poor man had found his way into this space was a confounding mystery. But it wasn't the only discovery to be made; beside the dead man sat several huge blocks of lead streaked with genuine silver.

The Psychiatrist

Chicago, IL

1885

"Are you ready to wake up?"

His eyes shot open and his heart skipped a beat in his chest. The woman's voice rang in his mind as if she has been mere centimeters from his ear, but after the initial confusion he always felt upon waking in such an abrupt manner, his senses returned to him and he knew no one accompanied him in his bed-chamber.

A recurring dream, it must have been, but the voice was so loud and so clear, it frightened him all the same. He would be awake for hours now, trying in vain to settle his racing heart and lull his thoughts back into a state of calm that would allow him to sleep again. Alas, he had been through it enough to know the effort was futile, and instead resigned to use the long nighttime hours to resume his studies in the library.

Dr. Nathaniel Martin considered himself extremely lucky to have chosen the field of psychiatry at such a remarkable time in the history of the profession. Educated men of his generation were ushering in a sea of positive changes to the field in an effort to classify, understand, and alleviate, if not entirely cure, mental ailments after decades of horrible rumors about the inhumane treatments at asylums across the United States and Europe. Not too long ago, such institutions were considered to be the only appropriate place to house "pauper lunatics," as they were often called. But at Nathaniel's hospital, The County Insane Asylum and Infirmary, he and his colleagues strived to make it a respectable alternative to incarceration for the mentally ill.

The city of Chicago had gone through a multitude of changes in the past ten years alone. New factories and mills had opened their doors to workers at a pace never seen in his lifetime and the city struggled to keep up with the demand for housing and medical care. The Chicago weather was unforgiving, to say the least, and so, too, were the conditions of the city's many poorhouses and prisons, the sole source of shelter for those who were too ill, in body or in mind, to work. This was the need Nathaniel's hospital promised to meet for the many who found themselves displaced in such a time of transition, and at the forefront of the city's progress was Dr. Nathaniel Martin himself.

He settled into his study, surrounded by heavy books, papers strewn across the desk, and the warm glow of a lantern as snow gently fell outside his window. He tried to read his favorite new text, an examination on the affects of alcoholism not just in the patients themselves, but in their relatives and ancestors. Though intrigued by its findings, he found his eyes to be too heavy from lack of sleep.

He picked up a stack of papers on the corner of his desk and perused through them: charcoal sketches he had done of various patients, a habit he had picked up during his residency. Nathaniel enjoyed his work, that was not to be doubted, but it could not be denied that the nature of it was, at times, quite stressful. For reasons unknown to him, sketching the patient's face while listening to their stories had a soothing effect on him. It was a way to see them that didn't involve too much eye contact, which made many of them feel distressed, as if they were animals being observed in a zoo. The conversation felt more natural and less like a science experiment, which in all honesty, it actually was.

A pang of sadness overcame him as he happened upon a sketch of one patient in particular: Charlie Winston, a troubled young man who had recently passed away after a fatal, self-inflicted overdose of chloroform. Who at the hospital could have been so careless as to allow a patient access to the usually locked medicine cabinet, Nathaniel could not say. Charlie looked back at him from the drawing, his eyes round, his face drooped, his hair starting to thin quite early for a man his age. A childhood filled with hardship and poverty had led Charlie's mental illness to become so severe it had consumed his every thought, both in waking life and in his subconscious dreams. Indeed, it had come to define the poor young man's entire personality.

Nathaniel grieved Charlie's decision to take his own life, but deep down, a part of himself could understand the patient's need to end his own suffering. The tragedy of it all was the hospital's failure - and indeed, the failure of Dr. Martin himself - to cure him in time.

He set down the pile of sketches, still at a loss as to how to wile away the hours until dawn, until an idea took hold of him: it had been far too long since he had written to his brother, Edward.

Oh, how Nathaniel admired his dear younger brother. Edward was nothing short of a genius. His skills as an architect had earned him the highest praise from city officials by the startlingly young age of twenty-five, and now, barely thirty, he had recently relocated to work for the premier architecture firm in New York.

Both brothers had done remarkably well for themselves considering their humble beginnings. Mother had been a beloved schoolteacher and Father had been the keeper of a bookshop near the University of Illinois. The shop's location attracted many scholars, most of whom Father befriended, and it was through these connections that both sons had been offered positions as students in their chosen fields after their father's untimely death.

Nathaniel had been but seventeen and Edward thirteen when their father passed from a terribly painful lung infection. The intervention of their father's acquaintances had been rather fortunate, but it was still the obligation of the elder brother to look after the younger from that point forward. Father had been a forward-thinking man who valued education and social progress, and though Edward took after their mother in likeness, Nathaniel saw a striking resemblance to their father in speech, mannerism, and sense of idealism.

Seated comfortably at his desk, Nathaniel composed a letter.

Dear Edward,

I should begin by informing you that Mother is doing well and continues to teach, even though I frequently remind her that she is welcome to retire and move in with me at any time. I am also doing well in my work at the hospital, although my troubled sleep continues to cause additional challenges to an already challenging work environment. I confess I have always been afraid of going to bed. Not of going to sleep, mind you, but of retiring to the darkness of my bedchamber and laying awake for hours.

Lately, I've been having the most puzzling recurring nightmare in which I hear a woman's voice speak so clearly in my ear, I can't help but wake up convinced she is in the room with me. Of course, she never is. Alas, I fear that I will not sleep again before the dawn, and will require a good amount of coffee to get me through my workday. But the work itself keeps me going, and for that I am fortunate.

Our city expands by the day, and I see workers come and go from the steel mills and factories at all hours of the day and night, sometimes in the vicious wind or snow, and I remind myself to be grateful for the occupation I have. Chicago misses you, as do I; however, I greatly look forward to visiting New York in the very near future to see a building my younger brother has contributed to its most magnificent skyline. Take care of yourself, brother. I look forward to a reply from you soon.

Ever Yours,
Nathaniel

* * *

The hospital could be a difficult place to work after a sleepless night, but Nathaniel persevered, as he always had. The insomnia was nothing new; in fact, he could remember sleepless nights as young as five years old. Even when he did manage to fall asleep, nightmares were not uncommon. As he approached adulthood and found himself with additional responsibilities after the death of his father and during his time at the University, the worry kept him awake even more. This had been a significant factor in his choice of psychiatry as his field of study; he desperately wanted to understand the underlying anxiety in his brain that provided such an obstacle to a normal circadian rhythm.

Sleep deprivation was not just a matter of feeling tired the following day. Over extended periods of time, it left Nathaniel feeling physically and mentally exhausted, as if his entire body were made of lead. It took a great deal of focus to force his brain to communicate with the rest of his body to move; his skin felt warm from an over-active heartbeat and his vision blurred almost to the point of feeling impaired by the effects of alcohol.

Nevertheless, Nathaniel managed to pry himself from the comfort of his sheets even after a mere hour or two of sleep, wash up, trim his beard and brush his hair, and dress respectably. He kept his spirits high as he checked his notes for the day over what was sure to be the first of many cups of coffee. The day did not seem to have anything unusual in store for him, just observational sessions with patients in various states of depression or grief, none of which, to his knowledge, had progressed to a full state of psychosis.

Dr. Martin approached the first patient's room: a teenage boy who had recently lost his father to a dreadful case of tuberculosis. But as he entered the room, he was startled to find the young man already being interviewed by a different psychiatrist.

The boy looked up with surprise at Dr. Martin's unintentional interruption, but the psychiatrist continued to look ahead, his back to the door, undisturbed by the noise behind him. Nathaniel mumbled a brief apology and quickly exited, puzzled by the mix-up in rooms.

The room next door, perhaps, was the one he should have entered. But upon his second attempt, he found himself in the same predicament: a boy, younger this time, maybe about eleven or twelve, also being interviewed by a separate psychiatrist with his back to the door. Again, the boy looked up, but the psychiatrist did not.

Baffled, Nathaniel stood still for a moment, overhearing a piece of the conversation that struck him as more of a lecture.

"Guilt can be a powerful motivator," the psychiatrist said to the child. "Perhaps this incident of losing him in the woods, and the feelings it has caused to rise within you, can be a reminder in the future that one must be more responsible, particularly with children younger than yourself."

Dr. Martin suddenly realized the impropriety of eavesdropping on such a conversation and left the room, gently shutting the door behind him. He shuffled through his notes, hoping to find once and for all where he needed to be and with which patient he was supposed to speak, but felt his confusion magnified when he couldn't seem to find any notes at all - the papers in his hands were all blank.

The loud bang of a door down the hall startled him, and when he looked up, he saw nothing but the long, white stretch of hallway with many heavy, locked doors on either side, but no exit.

Panic rising within him, he rushed to the end of the hallway - a dead end. He opened the first door he could see, hoping to find someone who could help explain to him where he possibly could have taken a wrong turn and how to get back to the hospital ward in which he belonged.

Instead, he happened upon yet another curious session, in which an unseen psychiatrist was speaking to a young boy - this time, a boy young enough to still be attending primary school.

"Remember what your father told you," said the psychiatrist. "You are the older brother and will one day become the man of the house, and the man of the house cannot afford to lose his temper this way. Your brother is not to be hit, no matter how frustrated you may be with him. He is younger and smaller than you are, and he needs you to look out for him."

Nathaniel stormed out of the room, slamming the door behind him. What in the Devil was going on? Professionalism, be damned - he had a right to know who these mysterious colleagues of his were and what kind of bizarre administrative mix-up had led to this situation.

With a newfound sense of righteousness, he stormed right back into the room.

"Good morning. Pardon the disturbance, but my name is Dr. Nathaniel Martin and I..." He trailed off when he realized the session was continuing in spite of his presence.

"Does it upset you to be responsible for Edward?" The psychiatrist asked.

Edward. Nathaniel's heart jumped into his throat when the stunning coincidences added up to the point that they could no longer be ignored. The oldest patient he had observed so far was being counseled after the death of his father due to tuberculosis - the same cause of death that had claimed the life of his own father at exactly that age. The second boy was rapt with guilt after losing a child younger than he, and the third was enduring a lecture on responsibility following a physical outburst toward a younger sibling similar to one his own father had given him at that age - a younger sibling named Edward.

The young boy looked up and locked eyes with Nathaniel. There was something strikingly familiar about him, though in the haze of so many misunderstandings, Nathaniel could hardly begin to deduce the reason why. And though Nathaniel could only speculate on the boy's inner thoughts at that moment, he couldn't shake the feeling that the boy recognized him, too.

Could this boy be a distant relative? Edward was a common name in his family, and if Dr. Martin had been assigned to speak with one of these patients, the discovery of a familial connection could absolutely have been the reason the patients had been re-assigned to someone else. But someone needed to answer him in order for him to get to the bottom of the issue.

"Excuse me!" he barked. Again, he received no response.

He exited the room in a huff, slamming the door behind him.

"Hello!" He shouted into the empty hall. "Can anyone hear me? Anyone?"

Silence.

He opened another door and found himself again intruding on the session with the teenage boy. He blinked. His head was beginning to feel woozy from the day's overwhelming amount of confusion.

He tried another door and found the young boy hearing the responsibility lecture.

He tried another and happened upon a fourth session: this time, the youngest boy yet, probably around the age of five.

"It is natural to be jealous of a sibling," the psychiatrist explained to him in a gentle tone. "You mustn't think you are unusual to feel that way about a new baby. Babies need a great deal of attention and you may be feeling left out now that your mother and father have him to tend to each day. But, Nathaniel, Edward is your flesh and blood, and attempting to give him to another family is not something you should consider again. Your brother is not like a toy you have grown tired of or a pair of shoes that no longer fit. Family is forever."

Nathaniel. Baby Edward. Family is forever.

Father had said the exact same thing to him when he was a child, jealous of his new baby brother and determined to reset the family dynamic to what it had been before Edward's presence had changed everything. Nathaniel, of course, had no idea the severity of his actions at the tender age of five, but nevertheless, the memory had haunted him and brought with it an almost unbearable sense of guilt well into his adult life.

He stormed out again, his head spinning, his palms sweating, his breath labored. The folder full of empty pages fell from his grasp and scattered across the floor. His entire body stiffened and his heart beat so quickly he felt as though it could shatter his ribs. He had seen many patients suffer from a psychotic break, but had never had the misfortune of experiencing one himself - until this moment.

Nathaniel fell to his knees and lost control of his lungs, only managing to breathe in heavy sobs, then collapsed onto his side against the cold tile floor. Ahead of him lay the never-ending white hallway and its many doors to nowhere. He was positively paralyzed with the desperate need to escape and the utter helplessness of not knowing how.

He lay there on the floor for what seemed like hours, staring into nothing, when his gaze finally landed on the empty papers.

But not all of them were empty anymore. Four of them contained sketches, done in Nathaniel's own penmanship, of the boys who were currently being interviewed. He slowly sat up and reached for them for closer inspection. Lining all four of them up side by side, the resemblance was obvious: each one was identical to how Nathaniel himself had looked at that respective age.

He found an ink tip pen in the pocket of his white coat and began furiously scribbling a letter to Edward for reasons he didn't fully understand.

Dearest Edward,

I write to you today from a most desperate place. I seem to be having some sort of psychotic episode, and though I cannot explain it even to my own satisfaction, I am overwhelmed with the feeling that my hallucinations, or whatever these visions may be, are somehow connected to my relationship with you. I carry much guilt in my heart for failing to be the older brother you deserved when we were children, and it is the greatest hope of my life that I have redeemed myself in looking out for you since Father passed. Now in the midst of a mental crisis, I find myself in need of the same sort of guidance and must ask for your help. If by the grace of God this message should find you, you must come to the hospital at once.

Nathaniel dropped the pen before bothering to sign his name. He was alone in this hallway, trapped like an animal, with none of his colleagues or patients, let alone a postman to retrieve the letter.

"Are you ready to wake up?"

A flash of energy bolted through his body like lightening. The woman was here, watching him, taunting him, perhaps even studying him. But where could she be?

He leapt to his feet and stormed back into a room, the one with the teenage boy.

"Where is she?!" Nathaniel cried. The psychiatrist seemed engrossed in his notes - rather, in the sketch he was composing of the teenage patient - and ignored him. "Tell me where she is, God damn it!"

Nathaniel lunged forward and grabbed the man by the shoulders, forcing him to turn around. He froze when he saw his own expressionless face staring back at him.

"You are the man of the house now, Nathaniel," his reflection said. "Your father prepared you for the inevitability of this day, and though it has come sooner than we would have hoped, it has arrived nonetheless."

"Why are you doing this?" Nathaniel cried to no one in particular. He backed up to the wall and buried his head in his hands. The gaze of his other self remained on him, unbroken.

"Are you ready to wake up?" the woman asked again.

"Tell me you heard her!" He yelled to both of the other men in the room. "You heard it! You must have!" They gave no reply.

"Nathaniel, can you hear me? Are you ready to wake up?"

He wanted to respond her, to ask her where she was, who she was, and why she would do this to him, but the words did not come. He slid down the wall, sobbing like a child, feeling his heart beat in his throat, and prayed that his mind would finally allow him to cry himself to sleep.

*　　*　　*

"Are you ready to wake up?"

Nathaniel's eyes opened slowly, and for a brief moment, his mind was entirely empty. A sense of calm washed over him, but it was immediately replaced by a sense of confusion. This was not his bed, nor even his home. The walls were bare and reflected the harsh afternoon sun into his eyes.

"There you are. Welcome back," said the voice. He sat up quickly and found himself eye to eye with a woman, about his own age, wearing a white coat over her simple blue dress, her hair tied up in a professional manner, with a notebook in her lap.

"Do you remember where you are?"

"No. What is this place?"

"You're at the hospital."

Nathaniel felt a sense of relief so strong he almost began to laugh. He had fallen asleep at the hospital and the visions had been nothing more than one of his nightmares.

"Oh, dear. I believe this is a first for me, falling asleep in the middle of a workday. I must apologize; this is deeply unprofessional of me."

The woman took a long pause before responding to him.

"Do you remember my name?"

"I'm afraid I do not, no."

"I'm Dr. Lindstrom, your psychiatrist. Please don't be alarmed, it often takes a moment for your memory to catch up when you come back."

"Come back?" He almost chuckled again. "Where have I been?"

"In a state of hypnosis. It has been a part of our work together for a few weeks now."

Although he was aware that many of his colleagues had recently begun to practice hypnosis with some of their more repressed patients, he had not been a part of it himself. A familiar feeling washed over him, similar to what he had felt in his nightmare. It wasn't just fear; it was far more painful than that. It was the feeling that the inside of his body was made of glass and could shatter at any moment. It was the feeling of slowly sliding toward a deep, dark pit of despair and knowing he would be powerless to keep himself from falling over the edge.

"Would you like to tell me what you saw? Was Edward there?"

"Edward?" How could she know about Edward? The question was silly, he knew that as soon as he thought of it. He had obviously told her about him, though he couldn't remember doing so.

"How about Charlie? Did you think about him?"

"Who?"

"Your patient, Charlie Winston."

It hurt to hear his name. Nathaniel's eyes welled up with tears so quickly it took him by surprise. There was something else eating away at him. The black pit of despair before him was not just one of depression or disappointment; it was also filled with grief.

Charlie Winston had recently died from a chloroform overdose in his hospital room. But as soon as Nathaniel thought of it, he knew in his heart that the story he had been telling himself was not correct. Charlie's death had not been a suicide. Rather, Nathaniel had attempted to subdue him during a manic episode and held the chemicals to Charlie's face for a second too long.

He remembered it clearly now, the moment Charlie's body went limp in his arms. He himself was culpable in the death of a man whose well-being was Nathaniel's own responsibility. He had not slept for days leading up to the tragedy and had spent the week drifting through the hospital halls like a ghost, trying his best to focus on his work but constantly feeling the weight of sheer exhaustion in every inch of his body, and in that crucial moment, had lost his focus in what he was doing, staring into the wall ahead of him as Charlie thrashed and squirmed under the weight of Nathaniel's grasp. When Nathaniel came to and realized where he was, the unintended damage had been done, and Charlie did not survive.

"Charlie. Oh, God. Charlie." Nathaniel buried his head in his hands.

"Was he there this time?"

Nathaniel shook his head.

"How about Edward? Did you revisit any memories of him?"

Her questions implied a connection between Edward and Charlie Winston, and he deeply dreaded the answer as to what one had to do with the other.

The pivotal moments Nathaniel had just revisited had all suggested he carried guilt for somehow having failed his younger brother, and he was a competent enough psychiatrist to know that such specific memories had to have been triggered by something extremely traumatic.

As he felt his emotions tumble into the pit, he slowly came face to face with the facts that hid inside of it.

Something was wrong with Edward.

Edward had been hurt.

Edward was dead.

* * *

Edward had brought his offer letter from the New York firm over to Nathaniel's home during their usual Friday evening supper. Nathaniel could not have been more delighted for his younger brother, but his jubilation was tempered by Edward's reluctance to take the job, explaining that he had recently met a most inspiring young woman from Virginia who had witnessed many deaths as a young child during the Civil War and had subsequently devoted her life to a career as a nurse.

"Her determination is like nothing I've witnessed before," Edward told Nathaniel, his round eyes sparkling. He was a very handsome man, clean-shaven and with excellent posture, but he had somehow managed to retain a boyish look about him due to his ever-curious nature. At least, that was how Nathaniel, who had always been and would always be the older sibling, saw him.

"She is entirely dedicated to the practice of medicine and retains such a lovely, warm sense of humor in the midst of so much suffering," Edward continued. "These are qualities I've always wanted in a future wife, and I intend to ask her to marry me. With your blessing, of course."

Nathaniel leaned back in his chair and carefully considered Edward's suggestion. Edward nervously drank more of his wine.

"Well, I applaud the young woman, of course, and I expect she will have many prospects for suitable spouses. But this offer is a once in a lifetime opportunity. Surely, there will be dozens of eligible women to choose from in New York, especially now that you are on your way to becoming one of the most successful architects in the country."

Edward nodded, avoiding eye contact. Nathaniel could read his brother's kind eyes better than anyone and knew he was feeling disappointed by Nathaniel's response, but not at all surprised.

"All I mean to say is, you have a bright future ahead in matters of finance and of romance. The best is most certainly yet to come." He gave a kind smile. "Whatever your decision, Father would be very proud of you, as am I."

Edward smiled in return. "Perhaps you are right." He raised his wine glass for a toast. "To the future."

Nathaniel raised his glass as well. "To the future."

Edward had been in New York for just over two months when it happened. He had been visiting the site of a condemned building in order to assess the property's potential for a new collection of townhomes in an up-and-coming neighborhood when the building collapsed. Three men were killed, including Edward, and two more were badly injured.

It was amidst this fog of grief and guilt that Nathaniel wandered in the bright labyrinth of the hospital hallways, the pain of his sleep deprivation radiating through his body, and had continued to work with patients like Charlie Winston, who paid the ultimate price for Nathaniel's state of mind on that awful day.

*　*　*

Nathaniel had been incredibly fortunate to only be stripped of his position at the hospital and not subjected to more serious consequences, but that was of little consolation. His punishment instead would be a lifetime of shame, doomed to fall on the other side of the glass, so to speak; a patient forever and a doctor no more.

Dr. Lindstrom looked at him with pity. It was the same expression Nathaniel had given to many of his own patients, and for the first time, he understood the humiliation of being on the receiving end of it.

"It is difficult to put these feelings into words," she told him, "but it is important that you try."

But there were no words to be spoken that could ever describe Nathaniel's pain. The mere thought of speaking to Dr. Lindstrom about it made him feel completely exhausted. All he wanted in the world was to sleep. To welcome the bliss of unconsciousness, a dimension where none of this was real and even the nightmares would be temporary and relatively harmless. But the realm of sleep was the last place his mind would allow him to be.

"Perhaps that's enough for today," Dr. Lindstrom said as she closed her notebook. "We can continue tomorrow."

Nathaniel was escorted back to his empty room with a wire cot and no window. It was a far cry from the warmth of his study. He desperately longed to be surrounded by his books and the glow of the lantern, comfortable and happy, tucked away from the chaos of life and the cold winter wind that tore through the city outside.

He lay down and longed for sleep. He could not remember the last time he woke feeling rested - certainly not since Edward's death, and perhaps not for days or even weeks prior to it.

Now here he was on the sterile cot in the empty room, doomed to a permanent state of confusion between being awake and being asleep, constantly wondering where his real pain ended and his nightmares began.

His mind raced with images of his last dinner with Edward, the emptiness of the hospital hallways, Charlie's dead body, laying on a slab in the morgue due to his own incompetence, and the four young versions of himself who sat alone in rooms exactly like this one, desperate to be relieved of the guilt each of them felt for failing

Edward in one way or another.

Exhaustion occasionally overtook him and allowed him to drift off, but his mind could not let go. He hallucinated waking up several times, sometimes at the hospital and sometimes in his own bed, but felt paralyzed and unable to move or speak.

This cycle continued for hours at a time, the false sense of waking life and the brain's constant attempts to keep him from full consciousness, lest he wake up and feel his heart break over and over again. All he could do was hope to again find his nightmares to be the result of his hypnotherapy and wait to hear Dr. Lindstrom's voice asking him if he was ready to wake up.

Acknowledgments

These stories would still be hypothetical ideations rolling around in my head if not for the love and encouragement of my family, friends, and creative community.

Thank you Mom, Dad, Robin, Krista, and Hannah for your continuous and unconditional love and support.

Thank you Hannah Park, Ian Gifford, and Elias Armao for sharing your artistic talent with me.

Thank you Mary Adams (a.k.a. Mom) for your dual role as cheerleader and copy editor.

Thank you to the many people who generously shared their time and wisdom with me during the writing and publishing processes: Liz Kerin, Angela Cohen, Alison Goodman, Monique Carmona, Jessica Kantor, Elise Sievert Bhushan, Sara Nesson, Ally Iseman, James Parris, Helenna Santos, Erica Brandon, Joe Carrillo, Robby DeVillez, M.G. Hall, Harry Hall, Megan Taylor, Connor Cook, A.D. Greer, Luke Zwanziger, Ruth Amos, Kristen Gorlitz, Ed Goto, Stephanie Ervin, Phil Popham, Patricia Selznick, Joey Adams, Darra Stone, Laura Coover, and Juliet Landau.

Even as a writer, I cannot properly express my immense gratitude for each and every one of you.

www.ingramcontent.com/pod-product-compliance
Lightning Source LLC
Chambersburg PA
CBHW011855300726

48970CB00009B/2812